"The program I built is tracing his and we should have a location on the latest victim any minute now," Bree said.

She tried to stand up but dizziness immediately assaulted her.

"Whoa, there," Tanner's arm wrapped around her, and a water bottle was lifted to her mouth.

"Did everybody make it out of the fire okay?"

It felt so good to rest against Tanner's chest as he pulled her against him. "Yes. He set the whole house to burn."

"We're going to catch him. What I was able to remember was more than enough."

He kissed her forehead. "You're spooky scary when that giant brain of yours gets going. Sexiest thing I've ever seen."

"Then how about we catch this guy and you take me to the hotel and show me exactly how sexy you think it is?"

"That would be my pleasure."

Bree's computer chirped. She pushed away from Tanner, ignoring the dizziness.

"That's it. We've got him."

"The program likely is racing its one
we should have a location on the least
victim any minute now," Jace said.

She tried to stand up but immediately plunged,
belted her.

"Whoa there," Jace said, "are you sure you should
be trying to get on the wasting to the shower?"

"Did you know how hard it can of me to..."

"Yeah, a good thing I caught her," Jace said,
"she offered me a sandwich," she said the while
it flew to him.

"We're going to catch him. Was I not able to
remember that more then any job."

She'd eaten her forehead. "They're obscene partly, right,
that they're planning our next comes. So wish back
I've been there."

"That's how much we caught this up and you take
me up the hotel and shop, relaxed." If we get you
out here.

"Thank you for my pleasure."

Every con ruler chance's Stir that led away for
behind through the corner.

"This is how we get him."

CONSTANT RISK

USA TODAY Bestselling Author

JANIE CROUCH

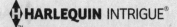

HARLEQUIN INTRIGUE®

This book is dedicated to Lissanne J. What a huge source of
support and encouragement you are—thank you! I look forward
to holding your own book in my hands soon.

ISBN-13: 978-1-335-64109-0

Constant Risk

Copyright © 2019 by Janie Crouch

Recycling programs
for this product may
not exist in your area.

Printed in U.S.A.

TM www.Harlequin.com

Janie Crouch has loved to read romance her whole life. This *USA TODAY* bestselling author cut her teeth on Harlequin Romance novels as a preteen, then moved on to a passion for romantic suspense as an adult. Janie lives with her husband and four children overseas. She enjoys traveling, long-distance running, movie watching, knitting and adventure/obstacle racing. You can find out more about her at janiecrouch.com.

Books by Janie Crouch

Harlequin Intrigue

The Risk Series: A Bree and Tanner Thriller

Calculated Risk
Security Risk
Constant Risk

Omega Sector: Under Siege

Daddy Defender
Protector's Instinct
Cease Fire

Omega Sector: Critical Response

Special Forces Savior
Fully Committed
Armored Attraction
Man of Action
Overwhelming Force
Battle Tested

Omega Sector

Infiltration
Countermeasures
Untraceable
Leverage

Primal Instinct

Visit the Author Profile page at Harlequin.com.

CAST OF CHARACTERS

Tanner Dempsey—Deputy captain of the sheriff's office in Grand County, Colorado. Lives and works in Risk Peak.

Bree Daniels—Shy computer genius, now living and working in Risk Peak, teaching computer classes at a women's shelter.

Michael Jeter—Head of a terrorist organization and the person who made Bree's life a living hell when she was growing up; currently awaiting trial for his crimes.

Noah Dempsey—Tanner's brother; they own a ranch together.

Cassandra Dempsey Martin—Tanner and Noah's sister; she runs the women's shelter in Risk Peak.

Richard Whitaker—Deputy of the Grand County sheriff's office; currently working in Dallas helping his colleagues with a serial killer case.

Penelope Brickman—Dallas PD detective in charge of the current serial killer case.

Jeremy Zimmer—Dallas PD computer specialist.

Gregory Lightfoot—One of the prosecuting attorneys in the Michael Jeter case. Working with Bree on her testimony.

Chapter One

"Here's the paperwork you need to look over, Mr. Jeter."

Michael Jeter barely noticed when the handcuffs pulled at the skin on his wrists as he reached for the piece of paper his lawyer, Beau O'Boyle, slid over to him. After the past five months of being in handcuffs regularly, he did not pay much attention to something that had irritated him to no end when he'd first been incarcerated.

There were many other things that irritated him to no end now.

The lack of flavor in all the food. The lack of quiet in the jail. And most definitely the lack of anything to do.

Up until five months ago, his hours had been filled from sunup to sundown running a worldwide, multifaceted charity that touched thousands of lives.

If that hadn't taken up enough of his time, the network he'd developed underneath said charity—where information, privacy and lives themselves could be sold to the highest bidder— certainly had filled his hours.

But now there were so many hours of *nothing*. Nothing to do but plan. And wait.

He looked at the paper, immediately spotting the code within the sentence structure that provided him with the real information he needed.

All messages, hidden or official, now had to be sent archaically—on paper. He didn't even like the feel of the parchment on his fingers. He much preferred a keyboard and screen. But he hadn't been allowed any sort of computer or internet access since the moment he was arrested. When Michael's lawyer came to see him, the man was required to leave every electronic item outside of the room.

It was almost as if law enforcement thought Michael would be able to vanish into thin air if he even came anywhere near any sort of computerized item. Like a computer-age Houdini.

In their defense, that wasn't totally untrue. If he had five minutes with a smartphone he could probably manipulate enough data to make the prison warden and guards think the wrong person had been arrested and maybe even let him out. After all, Michael was the most brilliant computer hacker on the planet.

Actually, no.

He was the *second* most brilliant computer hacker on the planet. The most brilliant hacker was the reason he was in jail to begin with.

For now.

Michael forced himself not to grimace at the feel of the paper as he continued to read. The encoded message was nothing less than he'd expected.

Michael read the letter again, a habit he developed around other people since his exceptional reading speed tended to make them uncomfortable. They thought he wasn't giving the document thorough attention since he finished so quickly. In this case it was probably better anyway. The second read through would allow him to almost memorize the info.

He looked over at his lawyer, unsure of how much the man was actually aware of. Almost everyone who'd been involved with the top tier of the Organization had been arrested. Anybody who was capable had immediately started flipping on others. That was to be expected. Loyalty dived out the window when the death penalty for treason entered the room.

Michael looked over at the lawyer. "Mr. O'Boyle, what exactly is your job here?"

His response would tell Michael everything he needed to know. Any response about law, the trial or the case would mean he didn't know the true contents of the letter.

"I am here to assist in all ways needed."

So, someone loyal. Good to know, not that they could talk openly about the real content of the message anyway. They were supposed to have a confidential conference room, but Michael was more than aware that Homeland Security was listening. He also knew there were cameras in this room right now surveilling what was written on the letter.

The most brilliant law enforcement minds in the country would be looking for encoded messages in it, starting immediately.

They wouldn't find any.

"Good to hear that." Michael held up the letter. "Thanks for the paperwork. Has there been any progress on the case in any other areas?"

"We are continuing to gather evidence for the trial. Things are going as best as can be expected."

"The cost is high. We have people willing to pay the price?" The security footage Homeland would run of this conversation would lead them to believe Michael was talking about the costs of trial preparation.

He was talking about something much different.

"Yes, sir. There are those who are loyal and

look at the bigger picture, willing to sacrifice short term, for the long-term good."

Michael gave a brief nod. "I'm glad to hear that is still true."

They had been prepared for this contingency. Perhaps not exactly in the way it had occurred—a young woman back from the dead taking them all down so swiftly and efficiently. That had definitely been unexpected. But from the beginning, the Organization had known there would be enemies, and that drastic methods might be needed to evade those enemies.

It was time for the drastic measures.

"What sort of schedule are we talking about?" he asked O'Boyle.

"The tentative court date is set two months from now. We can certainly push that back to give us more time to—"

Michael shook his head. "No. It's time to move forward."

He had plans of his own. Plans that couldn't be put into play until he was out of this hellhole of boredom.

O'Boyle nodded. "Of course. The trial itself could take weeks, which will give us plenty of time to continue gathering…data and anything else needed."

"No. I want to move forward now, not during the trial. Call the district attorney."

"But, sir..."

"Now, Mr. O'Boyle. Prison is inevitable for me. Let's not pretend it's not. I'm ready to not be in limbo any longer. I want to know my sentencing and move on with my life."

O'Boyle nodded. "Yes, sir. I'll start making the necessary calls today. But I must forewarn you, I think this might be a little premature. The closer we are to the end of your trial—"

"That will be all, Counselor." Michael didn't know if the man was unaware of law enforcement, who would be poring over their discussion, or if he'd momentarily forgotten. Either was unacceptable. "Make it happen."

Color leaked out of O'Boyle's face. "Yes, Mr. Jeter. It will take a little bit of time, but I can get the wheels set in motion immediately."

Wheels in motion. Good.

He'd been still for too damn long.

Chapter Two

"Remember that time when we were kids and Mrs. Ragan found that rattlesnake in her mailbox?"

Tanner Dempsey dragged his eyes up from the diner booth table to his brother, Noah, sitting across from him.

"Yeah, I remember. We were all terrified to get the mail all summer. Why?"

Noah grinned at him. "Because that's the same look you've got right now."

Tanner muttered a low curse and resisted the urge to flip his brother off like he would've done that summer of Mrs. Ragan's rattler. His eyes dropped back down to the small box on the table.

A ring box.

"I'm just saying what's in that box is not going to hurt you," Noah continued. "No snake is going to jump out of it. Or at least not a very big one."

Cheryl Andrews, owner of the Sunrise Diner with her husband, Dan, was making her way over with their lunch. Tanner quickly grabbed the box on the table. He definitely didn't want word to get out around Risk Peak that he had a ring box. That would spread like wildfire.

Noah was right. There were no rattlesnakes in the small jewelry case, just their mother's engagement ring. The one their father had given her when he'd asked her to marry him nearly forty years ago.

It was the ring he planned to present to Bree Daniels when he asked her to marry him.

"Did it bite you?" Noah whispered with a laugh as Tanner slipped it into his pocket.

Now Tanner did raise his middle finger, pretending like he was rubbing a spot on his cheek under his eye. He and Noah had been flipping each other off that way for so long that Noah immediately caught sight of the gesture and laughed.

So did Mrs. Andrews. "I'm going to pretend like I don't see you making rude gestures at your brother the same way you two have been for the past twenty years. I'd hate to have to call your mother down here to pick you up at your age."

"Yes, ma'am," Tanner muttered, dropping his hand immediately. He wasn't completely sure the older woman wouldn't actually follow through on that threat.

Tanner loved the town of Risk Peak, where he'd been born and raised. He loved it enough that except for the four years when he'd gone to college in Denver, he'd never even been tempted to leave. Loved it enough to have followed in his father's footsteps and joined the Grand County Sheriff's Department. Might even decide to run for sheriff someday.

This town had given him everything that was important to him, including Bree Daniels, the love of his life and hopefully soon-to-be fiancée.

She hadn't been born here like so many of the other residents. She'd shown up nearly eight months ago, broke, exhausted and hunted. When he'd caught her shoplifting at the town drugstore, stealing formula and diapers for twin babies who ended up not being her own, he would have never dreamed that she would become the woman he couldn't live without.

"Enjoy your meal, boys." Mrs. Andrews set the plates down on the table in front of them. "Noah, it's good to see you here."

Noah gave the older woman a nod. He didn't tend to come into town very often, preferring to stay out at the ranch he and Tanner owned together. Noah had his own house on one side of the property and Tanner, with Bree for the past three months, lived in a house on the other side of the two hundred and fifty acres.

Once Mrs. Andrews was gone, Tanner took a bite of his food. "Look, jackass, I only told you at all because Mom wanted to make sure it was okay with you that I use the ring. If you think you'll want it for whatever unfortunate sucker you talk into marrying you, then that's fine. I can pick out a different one."

Noah shoveled a forkful of the renowned Sunrise Diner meat loaf into his mouth. He was already shaking his head before Tanner even finished his sentence/insult. "Pretty sure marriage is not in the cards for me. So you go right ahead and use Mom's ring."

"You might be a little closer to marriage if you would actually date anyone."

Noah shrugged and kept eating. Tanner didn't push it. Noah had returned from his years as an Army Green Beret different than when he'd gone in. Stronger. Harder.

Colder.

His brother had never offered many details, and Tanner hadn't demanded them, but Tanner knew Noah had seen and done things in his time overseas that had changed him.

"So when are you going to ask Bree?" Noah said between bites.

"I'm not sure."

"Because you're trying to make it all romantic? You know stuff like that just stresses out your little brainiac."

Noah was right. Bree was a computer genius, but due to her upbringing—first within a terrorist organization, then almost completely alone and on the run—she wasn't great at interpersonal interaction. Normal things most people took for granted, like a conversation or casual touch, were often a challenge for her.

Tanner loved Bree *because* of this, not in spite of it.

"I'm only planning on asking a woman to marry me once. There's nothing wrong with wanting to make it special. I want to take her someplace romantic."

Noah shook his head and continued his lunch. "You do remember what happened last time you decided you were going to take Bree on a romantic holiday and make things perfect?"

Tanner rolled his eyes. "Considering I'm still recovering from my wounds and Bree barely made it out of that situation alive herself, yes, I remember it. And that's the exact reason why I need to make the proposal romantic and special. Get back up on the horse so to speak."

Bree had missed out on so much in her young life. She deserved a little romance. Deserved to travel and see somewhere besides a small town in Colorado.

"You know she loves the ranch more than anywhere else. Hell, brother, the woman just loves you."

"And I love her."

Noah shook his head. "Believe me, you two are so gooey, the whole town knows. Don't make the proposal more complicated than it needs to be."

They both finished their meal and pushed their plates toward the center of the booth. "I'm not making it complicated. I just want to make it perfect."

They both got up from the booth and walked over to pay the bill.

"It's on me," Noah said. "I want to be the one who buys you your last meal as a single man."

"I'm trying to keep this under wraps," Tanner muttered. "You know how the gossip mill is around here. I—"

Tanner stopped talking as Mrs. Andrews came back through the swinging kitchen door.

"You boys done?"

"Yes, ma'am," Noah said. "I'd like to buy my brother's lunch."

"How about lunch is on the house." Mrs. Andrews winked at them. "As long as Tanner doesn't take too long asking Bree to marry him."

Damn it.

He gave the older woman a tight smile. "I'm trying to keep that on the down low, Mrs. Andrews. I don't want Bree to figure it out."

"My lips are sealed. And you know Bree, this is all so new to her she'll never see it coming."

But was she ready? Tanner didn't have any

doubt about their love for each other, but was this the right time to even ask this of her? Maybe she needed more time. A chance to be on her own without anyone chasing after her, trying to trap or kill her. It was all she'd ever known.

Tanner was ready to start their forever right away, putting all that behind them.

"Where you heading now?"

"I'm supposed to meet Bree and Cassandra over at that abandoned office building on the south side of town."

"What are they doing over there?"

"Honestly, I'm not 100 percent sure. Bree just said Cassandra had a plan for expanding."

Noah looked at him with concern as they walked out of the diner.

"You don't think she's planning on having another baby, do you?"

Tanner shook his head. "It's our sister. Hell if I ever know what she means."

"I'm coming with you. In case you need backup."

Tanner chuckled. Cassandra had certainly talked the two of them into a number of stupid things over the years. Backup wasn't a ridiculous idea.

"Well, for God's sake don't mention the engagement ring to Cass," Tanner said. "You know how close she and Bree have gotten. And Cass definitely can't keep any sort of secret."

Tanner never would've thought that his sister and his hopefully soon-to-be fiancée would ever get along so well with one another, particularly after their rocky start a few months ago. Cass, when she found out about Bree's computer skills, had immediately demanded Bree teach computer classes at Risk Peak's women's shelter.

Bree had laughed at her.

Cassandra hadn't understood Bree's complicated history with computers. How she was both so good with them and terrified of them at the same time.

But Bree had agreed to try.

She might've been frightened to teach classes at the beginning, but there was no doubt she was incredibly talented when it came to sharing her skills with others. It had basically become her full-time job over the past few months. And Cassandra had become one of Bree's best friends.

Risk Peak was not that big, and it didn't take Tanner and Noah long to walk from the diner to the office building. The building itself had sat empty for nearly a year since the owner had died right at the end of construction, causing legal hassles as the property was left to his children, both of whom were going through a divorce.

Tanner had no idea what his sister could have planned here.

"There he is," Cassandra called out when he

and Noah entered. "And he brought my other favorite brother." Cass stepped closer to Bree and nudged her with her shoulder. "Probably because Tanner felt like he needed backup."

Cass and Noah immediately started joking with each other but Tanner ignored them. All he could see was Bree and her soft smile. He walked over to her and wrapped an arm around her waist.

"Hey," he whispered. Had it really just been a few hours since he'd seen her last? Noah was right. He did have it bad.

"Hey, yourself." She pressed closer. "I missed you."

"Cass is right though. I did bring Noah as backup. You never know what sort of craziness is going to result when Cass announces she has news."

Bree smiled. "This is pretty good news."

"Okay, lovebirds, keep it in your pants until you get home," Cass called out.

Tanner rolled his eyes, but stepped away—slightly—from Bree. "Mom didn't discipline you enough as a kid."

Cass hooked a hand on her hip. "That's because she was too busy chasing around after you two hooligans. Besides, I was an angel."

Everybody broke out in laughter at that.

"All right, so what is the big expansion surprise?" Tanner asked.

"This is," Bree said, stepping away from him and spinning around with one arm out.

"Are you guys going to open an office?" Noah asked.

Cass smiled. "No, even better. We've gotten a grant and approval to renovate this building and use it as a long-term women's shelter."

Tanner stepped away from her, looking around, trying to picture it. It wasn't difficult. Tear out some of the walls, add more bathrooms… The place was already in great structural shape overall.

But doing this would be a much-bigger commitment for Bree and Cassandra than the shelter. He looked over at Bree. "So someone will need to be living here full-time?"

Was that what she wanted? She seemed to love the ranch, but maybe it was too isolated for her. For the first time in her life she was starting to make friends. Maybe she didn't want to be thirty minutes away from the town and the people here.

"We're still working out the details of that," Cass said. "But the point is, we're going to be able to help a lot more women."

He wanted to argue, to ask for details, demand how this was going to fit into the life he'd been envisioning, but realized how unreasonable that would be. Especially given the excitement on both Bree's and Cassandra's faces.

Teaching these classes and helping these women was important to Bree. She knew what it was like to live in fear and not have many options.

Far be it from Tanner to try to limit her empowerment by stopping her from empowering others.

"I think it will work great," he finally said.

"Really?" Bree studied him, obviously picking up on some of his initial hesitation. "I think it could really be amazing."

"Absolutely." He gave her a nod.

"See? I told you." Cass said, turning to Noah and Tanner. "Bree didn't want to make any decisions until after Tanner had seen the building."

Tanner walked back over to Bree, feeling the engagement ring in his pocket as he reached to put his arm around her. If this was really what she wanted, maybe engagement was going to have to wait.

Maybe a long time.

Damn it. That wasn't what *he* wanted.

"What?" she whispered up to him as Cassandra started showing Noah how the space would be utilized. "What aren't you telling me? Do you think this is a bad idea?"

He hated the look of worry on her face. She'd already carried so many burdens and so much pain. He'd be damned if he was going to add to it.

"I promise I think this is a fantastic idea. I would tell you if I didn't."

She relaxed. After what they'd been through, she knew he wasn't going to start keeping the truth from her now.

And it was the truth. He did think this place was a fantastic idea. What Bree and Cassandra could create here would be amazing.

"I know you've got to get back to work," she whispered. "But I couldn't wait to show you this."

He wrapped his arm tightly around her waist. "And I'm so glad you did. You and Cass have a lot of decisions to make."

He did too. Just different ones than he'd been expecting.

Chapter Three

"When I was eight years old, I was invited to participate in a computer coding class provided for free by the charity Communication For All. My father died when I was just a baby and my mother worked really hard just to make ends meet. There were no finances for tutoring or extra lessons. Everyone, including my elementary school teachers, knew I needed to be challenged, but no one knew how to do it. By eight years old I had already figured out more than what most of them had learned in their computer science degrees."

Bree ran a hand over her eyes, then stared at the laptop screen in front of her on the kitchen table at Tanner's ranch house.

Gregory Lightfoot, one of the federal prosecuting attorneys for Michael Jeter's case, had been working with her two or three times a week for the past month on her witness statement for the prosecution.

Gregory was located in Dallas, where the federal trial against Jeter would take place. Eventually Bree would have to go there, but for right now they were working via teleconferencing. Her testimony in Jeter's trial in a couple months would play an important role. The case against the members of the Organization was very complicated and intertwined.

Bree wanted to help ensure the conviction of Michael Jeter, but this part wasn't the way she wanted to go about it.

She let out a sigh. "I just don't understand why I have to go back so far into my personal Bethany Ragan history. Why can't we just focus on me talking about the crimes I can prove Jeter and the Organization committed, and how I brought them down?"

As far as she was concerned, Bethany had ceased to exist once she'd gotten away from the Organization.

Gregory's face filled her screen. "Because what they did to you and your mother will be the nail in the coffin. Terrorist activities can sometimes be vague in a jury's mind. But picturing little eleven-year-old Bethany being tortured in order to get her to cooperate? That's the sort of thing that will guarantee a conviction."

"Right."

But did it matter that she didn't want to relive that? That there were times when she could still hear her own bones snapping in her dreams? That she could still remember what it was like to hold her mother as she vomited up blood from the beatings the Organization inflicted on her?

"Let's just focus on Michael Jeter," Gregory said. "Let's leave the more painful stuff out for today and focus on when you first met him."

Gregory didn't understand. It was *all* tied to Jeter. He'd been the face of her nightmares for nearly a dozen years. There was no separating him from the horror of what happened to her, even if most of it hadn't actually happened by his hand.

She attempted to focus.

"I moved up the ranks at Communication For All pretty quickly. At the time my mother didn't realize that the free courses were being utilized by the Organization to discover children who had natural hacking abilities. We just thought they were giving kids in poorer neighborhoods a leg up."

"And when did you meet Michael Jeter?"

"I'd been inside the Organization for over a year before that happened. He didn't get involved with the classroom programs in any regard except the highest possible levels. He met maybe one child per year."

"And you were that child?"

Bree nodded, glancing away from the screen.

"Yes. I'd aced every class and test they'd given me. I was already living on the Communication For All compound with my mom, and honestly was a little bored."

She could still almost perfectly remember the day she met Jeter. His office had been on a high floor in a Chicago skyscraper. She and her mother had grinned at each other all the way in the ride up the elevator.

"What happened at that meeting?" Gregory asked, yanking her out of the memory—one of the last clear good ones she had of her mother.

"I was brought into his office. It had unbelievable views from the window, and I wanted to look out them. But Jeter told me I had to do a test first before I could."

On the other end of the screen, Gregory jotted something down. "And what was the test?"

"To most people it would've looked like a computer coding game. That's how Michael presented it to me."

Thinking about it all now, with such hindsight, was difficult. If she hadn't wanted to show off so much, impress the bigwig in the fancy suit with the grandiose office, how much different her life would've turned out.

"I almost missed the true test," she finally murmured. "I was so used to everything coming so easily to me with computers that I almost missed the Trojan horse Jeter had put inside his little game."

The defect had been placed deep inside the coding, and couldn't be fixed with a simple re-write. Almost the entire program had to be re-fitted, and had to be done quickly and creatively because of the countdown the system was on.

"He was testing to see how I could adapt. He wanted to know what I would do when a system's walls started closing in around me. If I could think outside the coding box."

"And how did you do?"

"I passed." She said it with a shrug like it was no big deal.

It had been the hugest of deals.

She would never forget the look in Jeter's eye when she completed his little coding puzzle and turned the laptop back around toward him with time to spare.

Until that moment she'd been nothing to him. Just another kid who, with the right guidance, would probably grow up to do pretty advanced programming, or maybe even start her own busi-ness.

But once she'd turned the laptop back around to him and he'd seen what she'd done, she had become something much different to him.

Much more interesting.

From that day forward, until the day her mother

had finally broken them out, there wasn't a single day that Bree could remember that didn't have Michael Jeter in it.

"Were you aware of his illegal activities at the time?"

She let out a sigh. "I was eleven. And for the first time being challenged to my fullest potential. To me, it was all a game. In the beginning at least."

"And when did things take a turn for the worse?"

She stared at the screen, almost unable to focus on Gregory's friendly face. She tried to force words out of her mouth—once, twice—but they wouldn't come. Panic bubbled inside her.

All she could see was Michael Jeter.

All she could hear was his voice.

All she could feel was when her leg had been broken at his command.

The room began to close in on her, the past threatening to swallow her whole.

"Hey, freckles."

Tanner. She felt his hands on her shoulders, his strong thumbs moving gently up and down the back of her neck.

The terror faded. He was here and would help hold her demons at bay. She leaned her head back against his abdomen.

Without taking his hands off her, Tanner

crouched down so Gregory could see him in the screen.

"Hey, Tanner."

"Hi, Greg. Looks like we might need to take a break for tonight."

Frustration floated over the lawyer's features. "Being able to talk about this on the stand will make a difference in the case. Bree's already written it all out, so it's just a matter of being able to say it."

Tanner's voice was calm but firm, and his fingers never stopped rubbing her neck. "You read it, so you know what sort of trauma we're talking about. You're going to have to be more patient. Bree will get there, but it's going be on her timetable and nobody else's. And besides, if she decides she doesn't want to talk about all this, you're going to have to find a workaround. You've got plenty of other stuff."

Bree rubbed her eyes. She should be able to do this. "I'm sorry, Gregory…"

He held up a hand. "No, Tanner is right. You shouldn't push yourself too hard. God knows you've done enough to take the Organization, and Jeter, down."

"Some days it's easier to process the past than others."

"Well, like Tanner said, we've got plenty to go on even if we don't include details from your childhood." Gregory's voice dropped, and he gave her a sympathetic look. "But what he did to you so very clearly proves he's a monster. If we can use that to our advantage, I think we should."

Bree gave a tight smile and a nod, standing up and walking away from the table, as Tanner talked a few more moments with Gregory. She moved over to the front living room window, wrapping her arm around her midsection. She couldn't see anything in the darkness—dark came early here in the heart of winter—but her mind could perfectly envision the beauty of Tanner's ranch and the Rocky Mountains behind it. But right now the beloved scenery didn't help.

She knew Michael Jeter was a monster. She just didn't know if she could bear to relive it all.

Strong arms wrapped around her waist, and she leaned back into Tanner's strength once again. He didn't say anything or ask her to try to voice her feelings. And she loved him more for it.

"Seems like it's always one of our pasts coming back to haunt us," she finally said.

Just a few months ago, it had been someone from Tanner's past trying to hurt them. Now it seemed like it was back to being Bree's turn.

His arms tightened around her. "You stuck with me through my monsters. You can be damn sure I'll be doing the same for you with yours."

"I know it happened so long ago and I shouldn't

let it affect me now." She'd always thought herself so strong since she'd managed to survive on her own, but maybe that wasn't correct. "I'm not really a survivor. I'm just a victim on the move. I haven't really faced any of it."

"You're damn well not a victim, so I don't want to hear any of that talk." Tanner turned her in his arms so they were facing one another. "Just because you don't dwell on it doesn't mean you haven't faced it. So what if your mind balks at the thought of sharing the most horrendous details of your life with complete strangers. Nothing wrong with that."

"The thought of having to talk about this while Jeter is sitting right there in front of me? I'm just not sure I can do it."

He pulled her more firmly against his chest, tucking her head under his chin. His big body seemed to surround her on every side. It was almost impossible not to feel like he could defeat any foe for her when he held her like this.

"I'll be there with you every second you're on that stand. You won't have to look at him, you'll look at me. I may hate that bastard with a passion for what he did to you, but I'll always be thankful that, because of him, you ended up in Risk Peak."

He was right. Michael Jeter didn't have any control over her now. He was in jail, awaiting trial, and soon would be in prison. Probably forever. She didn't want to give Jeter any more of her time. Any more of her life.

She twined her arms around Tanner's neck. *This* was what was important. This man who meant everything to her. "Make love to me, Captain Hot Lips."

He grinned at her nickname for him. "My pleasure."

Immediately she found herself lifted by the hips and pressed into the window she'd just been looking out of.

There was no place for the ghosts of the past when all she could think about or feel was Tanner's strong body pressed up against hers.

This man had been her only lover, and it was just fine with her if that was the case for the rest of her life. She couldn't imagine she would ever find the same passion with someone else. And had no interest in trying.

Her head fell to the side, exposing her neck as those talented hot lips made their way down her jaw and onto her throat. She didn't even try to hide the whimper that escaped her when his hand slid up the outside of her thigh and hooked her leg over his hip. It brought them in direct contact with each other.

There was nowhere else she'd rather be than right here with him. She let out another little moan, pulling him closer.

"If you don't stop making those sounds, we are very definitely not going to make it to the bed," he said against her throat.

"Maybe I don't want to make it to the bed."

With a moan of his own, he reached down and grabbed her other leg so they were both wrapped around his waist.

They both let out a hiss at the build of the friction, the heat, the passion that was always just a breath away between them.

And no, they didn't make it to the bed.

Chapter Four

When Bree woke the next morning Tanner was already out of bed, which wasn't unusual—the man loved to wake with the dawn. She smelled coffee in the kitchen and padded from the bedroom to pour herself a cup.

Her heart stuttered in her chest as she caught sight of Tanner sitting in the rocking chair directly outside the window she'd been gazing out last night. He had a cup of coffee of his own resting on the porch railing.

When he'd been recovering from his stab wounds months ago they'd discovered that sitting out on the porch in the morning—even if it was only for a few minutes—helped settle his mind and get him ready for the day. His PTSD symptoms, a result of being held and tortured by a gang nearly four years ago now, were much easier to manage if he was able to take this quiet time in the morning.

She'd been wrong last night. She'd thought it

had been her mind's image of the land that had comforted her. But really it had been *this* image—Tanner looking out at the land that was so much a part of him him—that her mind had clung to. A strong, rugged man facing the strong, rugged land was the most breathtaking thing she'd ever seen.

She wrapped herself in a blanket and walked over and opened the door. His dazzling smile let her know she was more than welcome. She was almost to him when his arm just snaked out and wrapped around her waist, yanking her the rest of the way into his lap. His lips were cold against hers as he kissed her. She yelped and giggled.

"Good morning."

She wondered if her heart would do somersaults in her chest every time she heard his deep voice rumble in the morning.

She hoped so.

She fitted herself more firmly against him, curling her legs up onto his for warmth. His arms tucked her against him, pulling the blanket around her to keep her warm. A couple minutes later Corfu, the dog Tanner had given her months ago when she'd been heartbroken with loss, came wandering out of the barn and sat down contentedly at Tanner's feet.

"I don't think I could ever get tired of this view," she said, sipping on her coffee as he rocked them both.

His arms tightened around her. "Really? I would've thought you would want to see the world. Journey to all the places you never got to go because the Organization was hunting you."

"I will. There's lots of time to get to all those places." She smiled. "I'm not as old as you, you know—the Grim Reaper is not quite ringing my doorbell just yet. I've got plenty of time to see the places I want to see."

She expected him to tickle her or rub her back at the old-age comment, but he didn't.

Finally she nudged him. "Did I wear you out too much last night? Got you coming to grips with your own mortality? Do I need to go get your walker?"

Now she definitely expected him to pick her up and throw her over his shoulder and take her back to bed. Tanner might be ten years older than her, but he was definitely one of the fittest and most able-bodied people she knew. Their difference in age had never really been an issue.

"My job doesn't leave me a lot of time to journey the world," he finally said.

She tried to scoot back in his lap so she could look in his eye, but he kept her tucked up against him. "Well, I'm not planning on quitting my job and becoming a nomad. Now more than ever I want to be in Risk Peak."

"Because of the shelter?"

"New Journeys."

"What?" he asked.

"It's funny that you would mention traveling and journeys because that's what Cass and I decided to name the shelter in the grant proposal. New Journeys. That's what it is for so many of these women. A new start. A chance to go somewhere they've never been."

"It's a great name. And the new building…" He faded off.

Once again she was struck by his lack of enthusiasm. It was like he wanted to support this new change, but something was holding him back.

"I know it's going to be a lot of work, but I'm up to it."

"Believe me, I never doubted that you were up to it," he said.

She broke away from his hold and leaned back so she could look into his eyes. "Then what? Obviously there's more to what you're thinking."

He took in a deep breath. "Just, someone is going to need to live there, full-time, right? I thought you might want that."

She could feel her brows furrow as she tried to take in what he was saying. She'd been living here at the ranch since he'd gotten out of the hospital three months ago. It had started as her being here because he needed someone to help him recuperate. But, just like Tanner's mother had predicted, there'd been no talk of Bree ever moving back out again.

Until right now.

But maybe Mrs. Dempsey had been wrong. Maybe Tanner was ready to have his space back. Bree hadn't made any plans to live at the New Journeys building—she and Cassandra had already found a young, single mother who would make an excellent facilitator for the building. They'd approached Marilyn even before applying for the grant since neither Bree or Cassandra would be able to live at the shelter full-time.

Or so Bree had thought.

She knew Tanner loved her, and she loved him. But they'd never really talked about any specifics of how their relationship would play out long term.

"I—"

"Love doesn't—"

They both started speaking at the same time, then both stopped.

"You go," he said. "Love doesn't what? Say what you need to say."

Bree shrugged. She didn't want to make this awkward, although that seemed to be her superpower. "Love doesn't always mean marriage and settling down and having kids. I know that. I don't expect that."

It was what she wanted, sure, but she didn't

need a ring or a white dress to know that Tanner loved her.

She looked more closely at his face and realized she had said something very wrong. His features weren't cold, but they definitely lacked the warmth and welcome she'd always had from him.

She swallowed hard, a ball of dread forming in her belly. "Tanner, I'm sorry. I said something wrong, didn't I?" Damn her inability to process emotions like other people. "I love you."

Some of the cool melted from his brown eyes. He brought his thumb up and trailed it down her cheek. "I know you do, freckles. And I love you. I want you to be able to do all the things you want to do."

There was *nothing* she wanted to do without him. "There are things I want to do, but—"

Tanner muttered a soft curse as his phone began buzzing on the porch rail next to his coffee.

"Hold that thought," he muttered as he grabbed the phone. "I'm on call so I have to take this."

The way she'd already butchered this conversation it was probably best for them to completely restart it anyway.

"I'll go inside and start breakfast," she muttered, getting off his lap. He looked like he wanted to argue but the phone buzzed again so he just nodded.

Good. Maybe she could figure out how to fix what she was trying to say.

TANNER GRABBED HIS phone as he watched the woman he loved, the same woman who just said that love didn't equal marriage—bundle herself into her blanket and walk inside the house.

That talk hadn't gone the way he'd planned.

He hit the receive button with far more force than necessary. "Tanner Dempsey."

"Tanner, it's Richard Whitaker."

"Hey, Whitaker. I thought you were taking some vacation time and heading back to Dallas. Are you in Grand County already?" Whitaker was the other deputy captain of the Grand County Sheriff's Department.

"No, I actually just got off the phone with Sheriff Duggan. I'm going to be taking a little more leave, helping out here. Dallas has a serial killer, Tanner."

Tanner winced and gave a dry laugh at the same time. "You always did complain there wasn't enough action around here."

"Believe me, this particular case is more action than I ever wanted to deal with."

It almost seemed like the man was asking for his help. "You calling me for backup?"

Tanner couldn't imagine many scenarios where

he would be tremendously helpful for a murder investigation in Dallas.

"We do need help. In a big way." Whitaker's voice was strained. "This is personal for me. One of the victims was a girl from my old neighborhood."

Tanner straightened. He and Whitaker might not have always seen eye to eye, especially since a few months ago the man had thought Tanner was responsible for three murders, but Tanner would still do whatever he could to help him.

The fact that Whitaker was calling him at all spoke volumes.

"Richard, what do you need?"

"Actually, I need Bree. We're on a strict count-down—*literally*—and she may be the only one with the computer skills we need. The killer is sending live footage of the victim, and that's the only thing we've got to go on."

Tanner swallowed a curse. "That's messed up."

"I know. We're going to have another girl dead within a few days if we don't get someone in here who can think outside the box when it comes to tech stuff. I trust Bree, and we both know there's no one better in the world."

The only other possible person as good as Bree was currently waiting in jail in the city where he'd been assigned federal trial.

Dallas.

Tanner let out a curse. "You know Michael Jeter is being held in Dallas, right? I don't like the thought of bringing Bree into the same town as him, even if he is in a cell."

"I know, man. And trust me, if I had anyone else to ask, I would do it. We've got good computer people here, and they're stumped. We need the best."

That was Bree.

Tanner rubbed his eyes. Until Jeter was in actual prison, and not just a county jail cell, Tanner wasn't going to breathe easy, even from here. Bringing Bree closer to Jeter went against every protective fiber in his being.

But he also knew Bree. Knew she would never agree to hide from the possible risk of Jeter, even after her near panic attack last night just thinking about him, if lives were at stake. If Bree could help she would want to.

"Okay, I know she'll want to help. I'll get her to you."

He listened as Whitaker provided details about flights that day. Tanner would get Bree to Dallas. But he damn well would be staying glued to her side.

Chapter Five

On the way to help with a murder case was not the way Bree had envisioned taking her first airplane ride.

When Tanner had come in from talking on the phone his face had been pinched and tight.

"That was Whitaker. He's in Dallas and has a serial killer on his hands. He needs help."

She'd just nodded. She didn't like that their conversation would have to wait, but knew Tanner's job was always important. "When do you leave?"

"Actually, it's more *you* he needs than me. He has a killer sending some sort of live footage of the murder scene and their tech team can't figure out from where. He'd like for you to take a look."

She hadn't even been sure how to respond. The police wanted *her* to help with a case?

"You don't have to go, of course," Tanner said when she hadn't answered.

"No. I want to help." Just the thought of being at

a strange police department by herself, even with Whitaker around, was daunting. She shrugged. "I just don't do well with people. You know."

He pulled her against him. *Thank goodness.* Maybe she hadn't broken their relationship with what she'd said earlier. "I'm going to call the sheriff and get the time off so I can go with you. I wouldn't ever send you alone. Plus, it's in *Dallas*. I don't even like you being in the same state as Jeter, much less the same city. I don't care how locked up he is."

Tanner had arranged all the flights and details. He had even been excited for her when he'd realized this was her first time on a plane, taking the requisite picture of her from the airport terminal. He'd held her hand when the plane had hit a little turbulence. He'd talked to her and given her what few details he'd had about the situation.

Even though everything seemed okay on the surface, Bree knew it wasn't. Because of what she'd said this morning.

Score another point for the girl incapable of appropriate emotions. She didn't know how to make this right, and it wasn't going to get any easier while trying to help solve a murder.

Richard Whitaker was there to pick them up from the Dallas airport. He shook Tanner's hand and smiled at Bree, knowing her well enough to understand she wouldn't want to touch anyone unless she had to. She'd learned how to act appropriately around others, but it still didn't come naturally.

She gave him a little wave. "Hey, Whitaker."

"Thank you for coming." He walked with them out to his car.

"So what exactly is going on?" Tanner asked as they drove into downtown Dallas.

Whitaker took a deep breath. "We had two bodies on two different sides of town."

"What was the cause of death?" Tanner asked.

"They had both drowned."

"Are you sure that's even a serial killer?" Bree asked. "People can drown in just two inches of water."

"Believe me," Whitaker said. "I would not have brought you out if I wasn't sure we had a killer on our hands. Yes, the cause of death was drowning. Both victims weren't in water when they were found, but they had water in their lungs."

"Definitely drowned then," Bree muttered.

Whitaker nodded, keeping his eyes on the road. "They were both found in boxes—almost like coffins. Both were restrained in the box by both wrists and ankles."

"Someone filled it with water while they were trapped there?" Tanner said.

Whitaker nodded sharply. "Yes."

Tanner let out a curse. "Did you find out about them because of the footage the killer sent you?"

"No, that's new. Both victims were found by civilians. One in some woods off the highway about ten miles south of town. The other, Shelby Durrant, was found on the north side of town in a restaurant that had been closed for renovations."

"You know her?" Bree asked.

Whitaker shrugged. "Not very well, but we grew up near each other. She was ten years younger than me, so I never actually hung out with her. She was just one of the neighborhood kids, you know? She was still chained in that damn box when they found her."

He cleared his throat. Bree and Tanner both gave Whitaker a minute to collect himself.

"Any connection between the victims?" Tanner asked.

"Nothing that we've found so far. Both were female, about five foot three, roughly a hundred pounds. Shelby was twenty-two, an African American college student at Dallas Nursing Institute. Victim number two was in her mid-forties, Caucasian, married, with no kids. Her name was Kelly Quinn. She worked as a bank teller. Nothing we've been able to find ties them together in any way."

"What do you need me to do?" Bree asked.

Whitaker looked at his watch as they pulled

up in front of the Dallas police station. "That's going to become very obvious in about twenty-two minutes."

As they got out of the car she looked over at Tanner, but he just shrugged. Evidently he didn't know any more than her. Twenty-two minutes was oddly specific.

Whitaker signed them in at the front counter of the station and led them past a number of uniformed officers' desks to the back section of the building, where it was much quieter.

He opened a door leading out of those offices and everything changed.

People were buzzing around everywhere. This was obviously command central for the case. Multiple pictures of the two dead women hung on a large bulletin board. Some of them were from when they were alive. The others, definitely more painful to look at, were the bodies in those boxes Whitaker had told them about.

Dead.

They kept moving past the pictures into a large conference room. The entire back wall was made out of screens and had a half dozen computer terminals sitting right in front of them. At least ten people were surrounding the terminals.

Everybody was talking at once, vying to be heard. *This* was the situation Whitaker wanted her to work in? Even being in the general vicinity of this many strangers already had her cringing.

Her discomfort didn't get any better a few seconds later when a gorgeous blonde wearing jeans and a thin sweater—detective badge clipped on her belt—walked over to them.

"Whit," the beautiful woman said in, of course, a gorgeous smoky voice to match her perfect face and body. "Glad you're back. It's almost time."

The woman turned to Bree and Tanner, offering her hand. "Captain Dempsey, Miss Daniels, I'm Penelope Brickman, lead detective on this case. Thanks so much for coming."

Tanner shook her hand. "Hope we can help. Please, call me Tanner. Especially since I'm not here in any sort of official capacity."

Bree force herself to shake the woman's hand too. "Bree, please."

She was a little bit proud of herself for saying something appropriate rather than shoving all five feet eight inches of the woman's gorgeousness into a closet far away from Tanner.

"Did you catch them up?" Penelope asked Whitaker.

"Mostly. The footage… I figured that was just something they had to see for themselves."

Penelope nodded. "Yeah, explaining wouldn't do much good."

"How often does the footage arrive?" Bree

asked. "Is it live or prerecorded? I'm assuming it's been rerouted through multiple channels or you wouldn't need me here."

"I'll be the first to admit that I'm not any sort of computer expert." Penelope gave them both a rueful smile. "I can get around and do the basics with computers, but I tend more toward old-fashioned methods of solving crime and police work. Hitting the pavement and talking to people."

"I'm the same," Tanner said. "People tend to give up their secrets a lot more easily—"

"—than machines." They both finished together, then smiled.

Bree barely refrained from rolling her eyes. These two should just go get married and make a bunch of crime-fighting babies together. Babies, of course, who would never deign to touch the keys of a computer.

A yell at the front of the room caught their attention. The people at the computers were getting more frantic.

"What's going on?" Tanner asked.

"Everybody's on edge," Whitaker said. "It's almost time for the message. Every hour on the hour the bastard sends us some footage."

Every hour on the hour. That was the first completely useful bit of information Bree had received.

Without waiting to hear anything else, Bree

walked over to the computers. The people surrounding them were still talking all over each other, arguing about the best way to track the message that was coming in.

Bree just listened. Nothing coming out of their mouths was particularly complicated in terms of ideas on how to track the killer.

"Listen, people," the guy sitting at the main console said. "If we could catch this guy with any of those methods we would've damn well done so long before now. If you don't have something intelligent to say, then stand here quietly."

The group grumbled but quieted. Bree might not like how the guy was talking to everyone else but she definitely had to admit he was right. None of the ways they were suggesting were particularly inspiring.

The guy pointed at Bree. "Who are you?"

"I'm just observing for the moment."

"Great. Another useless person taking up space."

Bree ignored him. She might be pretty hesitant when it came to a lot of things—beautiful blondes included—but her confidence in her knowledge of computers was secure. She could probably do more than everyone in this room combined. But she had no need to prove that to anyone.

Yet.

"How long do you think it will be this time?"

the young woman next to her asked another woman sitting at a console.

"It was three and a half minutes last time. That was the longest so far. Maybe they will keep getting longer."

"But the time before that was only fifteen seconds," the first responded. "There doesn't seem to be any rhyme or reason to his methods."

A large digital clock on the wall beeped loudly and started counting down from thirty. Evidently the killer was punctual enough for them to set a clock to his transmissions.

Another good piece of information. That meant the footage was being sent on a computerized schedule, not just when the killer felt like it.

"Look alive, people," Mean Guy said as he sat down at the main computer terminal. "Remember we're still running all possible scenarios and solutions. Just because it didn't work one time doesn't mean it won't work this time. Everybody do your job."

Sure enough, right as the clock reached zero, every screen on the wall of monitors lit up.

The picture was just slightly blurry, enough to make it a little hazy. Bree wanted to ask if that was always the case, but didn't want to interrupt anyone from the jobs they were trying to do. The broadcasting window was limited. She could ask questions later.

The picture wasn't so blurry that you couldn't see what was going on. There was a woman restrained in a long, thin box. It looked almost like a clear coffin. The woman in the box was shown from the neck down. Her head was completely out of the shot. There was nothing distinguishing about the box itself.

Water was dripping into the box at the woman's feet in a regular, timed pattern. It had already filled a few inches of the container, but not enough to be very noticeable.

Something caught the woman's attention because she immediately began sobbing.

"Please! Help me please. Can you hear me? Please help me!"

Bree realized Tanner was next to her when he muttered a curse under his breath.

Bree's eyebrows furrowed. "Why does her voice sound funny?" she whispered to him.

"Bastard is using some sort of voice modulator."

That didn't make any sense to her, but neither did trapping a woman in some sort of coffin and slowly filling it up with water.

They had exactly twenty-three more seconds of the woman's hysterical crying before the feed completely cut off.

Bree looked over at Tanner, who looked as stunned as she felt, then glanced back around her.

"I should've been watching what they were doing rather than the screen." She pointed to the dozen people huddled around the multiple computers.

"It's hard to look away from something like that." Tanner reached over and squeezed her elbow. "And from what I understand, you only have to wait another fifty-nine minutes to get your chance and do it all over again. No wonder everyone here is such a mess."

Not having to wait long was a good thing. Footage coming in once an hour meant more opportunities for them to catch this guy.

"All right, people, sound off," Mean Guy said, like some NASA mission control simulation. "Tell me we got something."

"IP address was rerouted through multiple VPNs once again."

"Jumped to at least one public Wi-Fi, but not the same one as last time, so no triangulation."

"Top level was definitely utilizing a proxy server again. Encrypted coding."

With every announcement of unsuccessful attempts to home in on the killer, the group became more despondent. Mean Guy got shorter and shorter in his responses.

The blonde, Penelope, walked to the front of the room. She erased the number twelve from the whiteboard and wrote down thirteen, then turned to the people around her.

"I know you're tired. I know you're frustrated. We've been watching this happen for twelve hours now. I know seeing that woman suffering every single hour eats at all of us. But you need to focus. We've got less than an hour to have a new way of trying to catch this guy."

Mean Guy threw his hands up. "Triangulating his location just isn't possible. Whichever way we come at him from, he's already expecting it."

"Jeremy…" Penelope started.

"It's not impossible." Bree hadn't meant to cut off whatever Penelope had planned to tell mean Jeremy, but that had to be said.

"What?" Jeremy stood up from behind his computer and took a slight step toward Bree, eyes narrowed. She immediately felt Tanner shift a little closer, ready to step in, not that she thought Jeremy was going to hurt her.

She shrugged. "No offense—it's not impossible."

"Really?" he scoffed. "You've been here less than five minutes, saw twenty-three seconds of footage, and now you just know everything?" He turned back to Penelope. "No offense, boss, but this is not the sort of help we need."

Bree wasn't going to be cowed. Not about this. "*Impossible* is the term regular people use to make themselves feel safer about technology. To hide away from its fullest potential," she said softly. "And I knew that long before I walked in here today."

She'd learned it the hardest way possible when she was just a teenager.

Jeremy threw up his hands. "You think you can do better than we have? Be my guest."

A year ago, unable to read the interpersonal clues or tones, Bree would've thought that was an actual legitimate welcome to take over.

She leaned over toward Tanner. "I don't think he really meant that as an offer," she whispered. "I think he feels threatened by me. But I just want to help."

Tanner nodded and gave her a small smile. "He's frustrated. Everyone is. But they do want your help."

"Then I need everybody to get out of my way so I can get to work." She knew others could hear her, but it was the truth.

Jeremy let out a curse and a laugh.

Penelope cleared her throat. "People, this is Bree Daniels."

There was a slight murmur as her name was recognized.

"Yes, *that* Bree Daniels, who was responsible for bringing down Michael Jeter and the rest of the criminals hiding behind Communication For All," Penelope continued. "I daresay she might have some ideas we haven't thought of. So let's give her some room to work."

Jeremy walked over to Penelope and began arguing about something, but Bree wasn't paying any attention. She sat down in the seat Jeremy had vacated and pulled up what she needed on the system. It was time to go to work.

Nothing was impossible when it came to her and computers.

Chapter Six

Tanner walked away from Bree as soon as she sat down in front of the computer system. She wouldn't be aware of him—wouldn't be aware of almost anything—while she worked.

Whitaker caught his eye and motioned him over.

"Bree wasn't offended by Jeremy, was she? He's IT, not a cop, and he's pretty damn knowledgeable about computers. Dude can be a jerk, but in this case it's mostly frustration. Like Penelope said, for twelve hours we've been watching this poor girl lying in that damned box, terrified. The water's getting higher."

"How long do we have before it's critical?"

"In every single piece of footage that's been sent to us the water has been dripping at the exact same rate. Slightly faster than one drop per second. That means it's filling up at a rate of about one gallon every three hours."

Tanner did some quick math in his head. "So, around two and a half days before she drowns?"

"Could be closer to only two."

Tanner ran a hand over his eyes. "And your friend Shelby? Are you sure this was the same guy? There was no video of her, right?"

"No, thank God. I'm not sure I could've handled it. But the box was the same for her, as well as for the other dead woman. The general consensus right now is that they were some sort of warm-up."

"Or escalation," Tanner said. "Maybe he got bored killing them just for himself, decided to make it into a broadcast sport."

Whitaker grimaced. "Yeah, that's possible too."

Over his shoulder he could hear Bree demanding people move so she could work on two different computers at once. A few seconds later he turned around and she had all the different video segments up on the multiple monitors, playing in repeat, some two or more to a screen.

Even with no sound, it was jarring to watch the woman in the box. Bree stood for a long time, just staring at the monitors, taking it all in.

Penelope walked over to them and turned to the screens herself. "You guys have any idea what she's doing? We don't need her watching the footage—we need her figuring out where it's coming from."

Tanner gave a one-shouldered shrug. "Bree rarely does anything without a purpose. If she's studying the footage, it's because she thinks it will help her."

Penelope crossed her arms over her chest. "Fine. But we've got less than forty-five minutes until the next live stream. She needs to be ready."

Tanner turned away from the monitor. "Believe me. Bree will be ready. That clock you have running the countdown? She won't need it. Her brain is already keeping completely accurate track of the time without her even trying."

Because that's how Bree's brain worked. The things most people had to put conscious effort into, it did automatically.

Like a computer.

Penelope nodded. "Good, because like Jeremy said, our team thinks this guy can't be traced."

"If it's possible, Bree will do it," Whitaker said.

"And she'll do it faster than anyone," Tanner finished for him.

Penelope didn't look convinced, and Tanner couldn't blame her. Bree was young, not very polished, and most people were going to underestimate her for that.

"I can't help with computer stuff, but I'd be happy to be an extra set of eyes and ears for anything else, if you don't mind my involvement." Tanner didn't want to step on any toes. Some departments liked to keep investigations as close to the vest as possible.

Evidently Penelope wasn't one of those types of leaders. She nodded. "I'll take every eye on this we can get. Maybe you'll see something we're missing. Because I'm damn tired of sitting here waiting for the top of each hour to come by just for us to be toyed with again."

They sat down at the conference table and Whitaker pulled up a link.

"These are the twelve live streams in the order in which we received them. All in all, it's a little bit less than fifteen minutes of footage."

Tanner played each one so he could get an understanding of the full scope, then immediately started watching again, this time pausing whenever he needed to in order to study details.

The killer never showed up in a single shot. The camera never panned or zoomed—never moved at all.

"The room isn't very big," Tanner said. "I would think the camera is mounted over the door."

Whitaker leaned over his shoulder to look at the footage.

"I agree." Penelope sat down next to him. "We can't see the woman's face, but we think that there's some sort of light on the camera that switches on when it's transmitting."

Tanner nodded, skipping to footage number four and pointing to the screen. "Yes. Because she's inactive for a few moments and then sees whatever she sees, and that's when she starts begging for help. So she's probably not blindfolded."

He skipped ahead to the other footage, pointing out where she did the same thing.

"Right," Penelope said. "And sometimes she doesn't seem to see anything at all. Maybe she's sleeping?"

Tanner and Whitaker both nodded. "There are no windows in the room," Whitaker said. "The light is always constant. She probably has no idea if it's day or night."

Tanner nodded. "And who knows how long this bastard held her before he even started sending the footage."

"She's definitely more hysterical in some of the recordings than others." Penelope put her hand over Tanner's on the mouse, then glanced at him. "Do you mind if I…"

He moved his hand. "Be my guest."

She clicked so that five different images took up the screen. "These were when she was most hysterical. Already sobbing before the live stream even came through."

Tanner watched each separate clip. Penelope was definitely right. The woman was already crying when the footage started, not because she realized the camera was on.

Listening to her—fear and desperation so close to the surface—was agonizing.

Tanner muttered a curse. "Is there any pattern that we see? Are there clips where she's upset longer? Is he hurting her and wanting us to see it? I don't see any markings on her body to indicate he's hurt her."

"No," Whitaker said. "When it first happened we thought maybe he was escalating. That the clips would get longer as he got more violent, or show her harmed, but that hasn't happened. And there doesn't seem to be any pattern to how long the clips run."

"She'll be hysterical one hour then much better the next, thank God." Penelope rubbed her eyes with her fingers. "I've watched these clips over a hundred times. Whit has also. But we haven't found anything that helps at all."

"Just makes me pretty damn furious," Whitaker said.

Jeremy walked over to them. "We're up in less than three minutes, boss."

Penelope nodded. "Any progress over there?"

"Bree isn't saying very much, but she seems to know her stuff, which isn't surprising, given who she is. This will be the first time she's seeing what's happening behind the scenes as the footage comes in. No offense, but I don't think she'll be quite so quick to say *no such thing as impossible* after she really understands what's going on."

"Give her a chance," Penelope said.

Jeremy shrugged. "At this point I'm willing to give anybody a chance. I just don't want us putting all our eggs in one basket. Plus, she's not making any friends over there."

"Why? What happened?" Penelope asked, as they all stood.

"One of the first things she did was set up a program so it records what's happening on everyone's computer screen. Bree said she wanted to be able to look over what everyone was doing in case they missed anything."

Whitaker looked over at Tanner and they both winced. People who didn't know Bree wouldn't understand the kindness and gentleness that resided under her sometimes-abrupt exterior. Her actions would seem like she thought herself superior to everyone else.

They walked over to the monitor screens to prepare for the next transmission. Bree had made herself a little command center and was typing on one keyboard as her eyes darted back and forth between three screens.

Tanner walked over to stand right behind her. "I don't have anything yet," she said without looking at him. "There's something weird going on that I haven't been able to put my finger on."

He rubbed the back of her shoulders. "Nobody expected you to come in and solve this in an hour. Let's give it a little more time."

Her disgusted grunt told him she had in fact expected to be able to solve this in an hour.

Just a few seconds later, the countdown clock began to beep. Bree didn't even look up from her monitor.

The crying, sounding even more eerie because of the voice modulator, came through just a split second before the video did. The video was exactly the same as all the others. Nothing could be seen but the coffin-sized box containing the woman from the neck down. She was struggling against the metal cuffs that attached her wrists and ankles to the sides.

Everyone's attention was riveted to the screens in front of them, except Bree.

Even when the woman was sobbing and begging to be freed—this was obviously not one of her good moments—Bree didn't look up from what she was doing. Besides the crying, Bree's fingers on the keyboard were the only thing that could be heard.

Tanner understood Bree well enough to know what was going on. She knew the victim was not the key to finding the location to where she was being kept. The key was in figuring out the details of the transmission.

But to everybody else it looked like Bree didn't care at all about the suffering of this poor woman. Like Bree couldn't be bothered to stop typing for the seconds the transmission would last and at least acknowledge the woman's misery.

The transmission ended as suddenly as it began. Bree's hands never stopped moving on the keyboard. Nearly everyone in the room was staring at her, the noise from her fingers sounding throughout the room. Tanner was glad Bree was caught in her own world and had no comprehension of what was going on around her.

"Do you mind if we play it again, Bree?" Penelope finally asked.

"Would hate to disrupt you in any way," Jeremy muttered.

Bree didn't even look up. "That's fine. The victim is irrelevant."

Even Tanner had to wince a little at that one. Jeremy rolled his eyes and walked over to one of the computers and set the footage to play again.

"Okay, people, what do we see?" Penelope asked when it was done.

"She was already crying before the camera turned on. It was one of the times when she seemed not to be aware of the transmission at all," Whitaker said.

"All right, so it's one of her bad hours. Maybe she's tired. Maybe he hurt her." Penelope had them play the footage again.

There were so many things that could be happening to the poor woman to make her hysterical.

Hearing the modulated crying caused Tanner to look more closely at the screen. He walked over and stood next to Whitaker. "Your friend Shelby and the other victim."

"Kelly Quinn," Whitaker filled in for him.

"You didn't find any links between them?"

"Nothing of any significance."

"Did you check where they shop for clothes? They were both similar build, right? I know we don't have great perspective from this footage, but looking at this new woman, she could possibly be about the same size also. Relatively petite. Slender."

"Definitely worth a try." Whitaker called Penelope over and she agreed it was worth redoubling their efforts to see if it led anywhere, and immediately got someone on it.

They played the footage again and Tanner stepped closer to the screens. The crying was so much more jarring with a voice regulator distorting it.

The killer wasn't letting them see her face and wasn't letting them hear her real voice.

Why?

Tanner looked over at Whitaker and Penelope. "You guys got any local celebrities missing or anything?"

Penelope raised an eyebrow. "Not that I've heard. Why?"

Tanner shrugged. "Just seems like an awful lot of work to use a voice modulator when we can't see the victim's face anyway. Leads me to think there might be something about her voice that's unique. Something we'd recognize right off if we could see or hear her clearly."

Whitaker muttered a curse. "You're right. I can't believe we didn't think of that."

Tanner slapped him on the shoulder. "Trying to figure out who framed me for murder gave me a better perspective on thinking outside the box."

Whitaker had the good grace to look sheepish, since he'd been the person most convinced Tanner was guilty. "I'm glad something good came out of that."

Penelope played the clip again. "Damn it. I think you're right, Tanner. I haven't heard anything about a well-known missing person, but we'll put some feelers out immediately. But knowing the victim still isn't going to help us get to her. We need the location."

"Give Bree time," he told her.

BREE WORKED ALL night long on the tracking without stopping.

Whitaker and another one of the detectives on the case, Leon Goulding, an African American man in his late twenties who'd joined the Dallas PD after Whitaker left, took Tanner to show him where the first two victims had been found.

None of them had found anything useful in either the woods or the empty restaurant, but at least it had given Tanner a frame of reference.

Then they'd taken him to the evidence room and shown him the boxes the dead women had been found in—identical to the one the woman from the footage was currently trapped in. The boxes were lying on a table side by side.

"They're made of low-density polyethylene," Leon said as Tanner walked around looking at them. "Basically the same thing trash cans are made from."

Tanner nodded. "So they definitely wouldn't have any problem holding water."

Whitaker was studying the boxes too. "That's correct. We even filled one of them to capacity to double-check. The seams are reinforced with an acrylic binder."

Tanner took a closer look. "Like an aquarium."

"Yes, exactly," Leon said. "These boxes are the same size down to the millimeter, and as best we can tell, are pretty damn close to the size of the box in the footage."

Tanner looked at the length of them. "There's no way an average-sized man could fit in one of those. I think the killer might be choosing his victims based solely on their size."

Whitaker nodded. "Body shape and size was the only thing we've been able to find in common between Shelby and Kelly Quinn."

Tanner rubbed the back of his neck walking around the table. "He's building a new box for each victim rather than reusing the one he has."

"What does that mean?" Leon asked.

"I think the killer wants to be able to know the exact minute the victim will drown. He wants to control everything about her death. Control is his MO, and he's left nothing to chance."

The footage continued to arrive at the top of every hour all night also.

They went through twelve cycles, some where the woman was relatively calm, some where she was hysterical. Then, most disturbing, some when she began to realize the water dripping so slowly on her was eventually going to be what killed her.

She didn't talk about that realization in every transmission, but when she did, it was heartbreaking. She wasn't hysterical, wasn't crying.

Just a whispered question. "The water. How

long will it take before it fills up?" Like she was trying to work it out in her mind.

She'd mentioned the water three times in the last twelve hours. Almost like she was resigning herself to her fate. That was the last thing they wanted. The woman giving up hope would kill her quicker than anything.

Tanner had even caught Bree watching that footage with a frown—if Bree was stopping what she was doing to watch, that definitely meant it was pretty bad.

Somebody played the last clip again. Tanner couldn't help but flinch as the woman talked about the water in her stoic voice.

Penelope came and stood next to him, offering him a cup of coffee. "Any idea how long before Bree might possibly have an update?"

"As soon as she knows something definitive, Bree will say. Asking her for updates now just slows her down." He gestured toward the screen. "I know this feels pretty bleak, but we should have at least another thirty-six hours before that damn thing fills with water, right?"

"Actually, drowning is the best-case scenario. We consulted with a medical professional and unless that water temperature is carefully regulated she could die of hypothermia before she drowns."

Tanner let out a curse. "So how long do we have?"I

"Doc says she's not showing any signs of hypothermia yet from what he can tell in the latest footage, so that's good. But as the water gets deeper…"

Tanner glanced over at Bree. "I can ask her for an update, but I promise she's working as hard as she can. Bree only has one speed when it comes to this sort of thing, and believe me, it's faster than you and I and probably everyone else in this room put together. As soon as she's got something she'll let us know."

Penelope looked as if she was about to argue the point when Bree called out behind him.

"I've got something!"

Everyone got quiet. Tanner just smiled.

Chapter Seven

The bastard was smart, Bree would give him that. She walked toward Tanner, frowning when she saw him talking to the beautiful blonde woman whose name she couldn't remember, even though she'd said it when they'd met, however many hours ago. The detective in charge.

Blondie looked excited. "You located the victim?"

Bree shook her head. "Not yet."

She looked around and realized everyone was staring at her and grimaced. She never liked to be the center of attention. She felt better when Tanner slipped his arm around her.

Talking to Tanner was easier, so Bree focused on him. "The guy is using multiple VPNs and proxy servers to hide the actual location of where he's streaming from. Bouncing it around all over the place but keeping it local enough that I wouldn't question it or eliminate it completely."

Jeremy walked over, nodding. "That's what I was trying to tell you from the beginning."

Bree looked over at him. "And you were right. There's no way to track the killer that way."

"Then what exactly is your breakthrough?" Blondie asked.

"I'm sorry, what's your name again?"

"Penelope." She arched an eyebrow. "I am the detective in charge of the case."

Bree nodded. "Right. Penelope. I know. I'm sorry, I'm not very good with names. It was actually the victim herself who got me thinking in the right direction."

Jeremy rolled his eyes. "I didn't think you were even aware there was a victim given how little you paid attention to her."

Bree winced.

"Enough, Jeremy," Whitaker said from the conference table.

Tanner's arm tightened around her, but Jeremy was right. Bree hadn't been even remotely as focused on the victim as she had been the computer side of things. She could've at least been a little more sympathetic.

"You're doing fine," Tanner whispered in her ear. "Everybody here has a job, and yours was to focus on the transmissions."

Everybody else had a job also, and yet had somehow managed to be sympathetic to the plight of the woman. Everyone except Bree. She rubbed her fingers over her eyes. "Right. Well, the woman started talking about the water."

"And?" Penelope said. "You got something from that?"

"My brain just picked out that she seemed to be talking about it every fourth set of footage."

Penelope looked at Whitaker and then over at Tanner. "Is that right?"

Jeremy pulled up the footage and played the last twelve transmissions.

"I'll be damned," Penelope muttered. "She does talk about the water every fourth one. Do you think she's trying to signal us?"

Bree shrugged. "Honestly, I have no idea what she's doing. I can't even imagine what goes through someone's mind if they're trapped like that. The pattern of it just got me thinking in a different way."

"So, her mentioning the water didn't have anything to do with whatever it is you've come up with?" Whitaker asked.

Bree shook her head. "No, not at all. It just got me started on looking for patterns, rather than taking all the footage holistically."

Penelope rubbed her hand over her eyes. "Can somebody please tell me what she's talking about?"

They didn't understand. Bree turned to Tanner instead. "I found a fractal pattern in the transmissions."

He probably didn't understand either, but at least Tanner nodded. "How does that help us?"

"It means that every fourth time there's something a little bit different with how the killer is transmitting. Those times it's a self-similar pattern with expanding symmetry."

Penelope snapped to attention. "Is the woman trying to tell us that by talking about the water."

Bree shook her head. "No. There's no way she could know about it. I thought the transmissions were random, but not all of them are. This is something he overlooked, or thought we wouldn't discover."

"Okay," Tanner said. "How does it help us?"

"I can use it to catch him. I don't have to track *him*, just find the system using the fractal pattern. It's very specific. But I can only do it every fourth transmission, and it has to be while the transmission is live."

"But now you know what you're looking for," Tanner said.

She reached up and squeezed his bicep. He understood. Tanner always understood. "Yes. Now that I know what it is, it's just a matter of time. I might not be able to get you to the actual room, but I'll be able to get you pretty damn close."

Whitaker walked over and squeezed her shoulder. "You get us close, we'll do the rest."

"I can't do anything for another three hours. That's when the next transmission that's using the fractal pattern will go live."

"How many more footage segments do you need?" Tanner asked.

"The next one will get us close, but I can't guarantee exactly how close. We'll need to be ready to move to where that one leads. Then I'll need at least one more after that to pinpoint."

"There's nothing you can do with any of the other footage segments? No clues there?" Penelope asked. "You're saying we're at least seven hours and possibly eleven or more before we have actionable intel?"

Bree shrugged. "Yes. I can't work any faster than the pattern he submits on."

Penelope shook her head. "That's too long. The victim might not even be alive at that point."

Bree blinked a few times and looked over at Tanner. "I haven't worked out the exact math in my head, but it seems like she should have at least thirty-six more hours before the water covers her. Is my math off?"

His arm slipped back around her waist. "That's correct, but medical experts are concerned about hypothermia."

"Unless that water is temperature controlled, she could die," Whitaker said.

What was Bree supposed to do? She couldn't magically make the pattern work more quickly. "I'm sorry. This anomaly in how the footage is being transmitted is only occurring every fourth time. I can't change that or speed it up."

"If he made an error in whatever he did with every fourth set of footage, maybe he made an error somewhere else," Penelope said. "We just need to find it. And we need to do it now."

Translation: *Bree* needed to find it.

Bree nodded. "Let me write the pattern recognition program I'll need to trace him when the next flawed transmission comes in. Then I'll do my best to see if I can find any mistakes in the other transmissions."

Without another word, Bree turned away from them all, giving Tanner's hand a squeeze as she did. She'd been working on this for twelve hours. She'd already looked for any mistakes the killer might have made and hadn't found anything.

She wrote the program and had it ready to go, then spent the next two hours searching for another needle in the haystack. At every top of the hour when new footage came in she ran it against the pattern recognition program she'd written, but nothing showed up. She wasn't surprised. The fractal pattern was damn near brilliant and it was just sheer luck she'd discovered it. If he was using something similar for his other transmissions, Bree couldn't spot it.

She was also tired, and working at a pace her brain wasn't used to. At one time, thanks to Jeter threatening physical harm to her or her mom, she'd been able to work at this pace for days at a time.

Not being tortured for the past ten years had caused her brain to get lazy.

She was tired, wanted to rest. Plus, every time she looked over at Tanner, beautiful, blonde Penelope with all her appropriate emotional reactions was next to him. By all accounts Penelope had been here over twenty-four hours. Who looked that good after working twenty-four hours straight?

Bree caught her own reflection in the monitor. She didn't look good, that was for sure. But she didn't even try to fix the messy bun she'd piled her hair into. What would be the use. She had a pen resting behind either ear. Both of which she'd been looking for but hadn't been able to find.

She was a mess. But attempting to fix her hair wasn't going to change that.

They were twenty minutes from the transmission Bree needed to help pinpoint the killer when she heard a phone buzzing on a desk nearby. She waited for someone to pick it up before she realized it was hers.

When she glanced at the screen and saw it was Gregory Lightfoot, she almost let it go to voice mail. But the lawyer would just call back, and in a few minutes hopefully they would be on the road on the way to catch the killer. She might not be available.

"Lightfoot. I don't have a lot of time I'm helping the police."

"Good morning to you too, Bree," Gregory said good-naturedly.

She cringed. "Sorry. All my people skills have already been used up." Such as they were.

He chuckled. "I'll keep this short, and hopefully this will be good news. Michael Jeter took a plea bargain."

Bree's hand raised to her throat and her heart rate kicked up. "What sort of plea bargain?"

Surely they wouldn't let him out of jail. Would they? She felt like the room was closing in on her—the air being sucked out.

"Freckles, what's wrong?"

She turned her head and found Tanner crouching on the floor beside her so his face was at the same height as hers.

She grabbed his hand. "Jeter made some sort of deal."

She turned the phone so Tanner could also hear what Gregory was saying. She didn't want to put it on speaker in front of all these people.

"Lightfoot, what's going on?" Tanner asked.

"It's good news, I promise. Yes, Jeter plea-bargained, but only to take the death penalty off the table. He'll be serving four life sentences without the possibility of parole."

Her eyes met Tanner's deep brown ones. "He won't ever be able to get out of prison?"

"Never," Gregory assured her. "I think Jeter knew he was going to get the death penalty, so this was the best play he had. But he's never getting out of prison, I can promise you that."

"Where will he do his time?" Tanner asked.

"That's a little bit more complicated. They're transferring him tomorrow to the federal prison in Beaumont. He'll be there probably three to six months until the details are finalized."

Tanner nodded and it reassured Bree—if Tanner was happy about him being at Beaumont then that meant it was a good place for Jeter to be.

"That's a solid max security. Definitely better than the county jail he's been in," Tanner said.

"Best of all, this solves all your testimony problems, Bree. You're not going to have to take the stand at all."

Finally, some good news.

She promised to contact Gregory for more details as soon as this case was done and she was back home, and ended the call. Right now she needed to focus on catching an entirely different bastard.

Tanner squeezed her hand. "You okay?"

She shrugged. "Honestly, I don't know. I just

need time to process this. But that will have to wait until I'm done here. I'd rather stick with this. Computers, I know. Feelings are much more complicated."

He kissed the top of her head. "Anyone would need time to sort this out, so don't feel bad about that. Do you have everything ready for the next transmission?"

"Yes. I'm sorry I couldn't find anything to make this quicker."

He pulled her against him and kissed her hard and brief. "You found the pattern. That's more than anyone else did. We're going to catch this guy and we're going to be in time to save this woman. Because of you."

"Because of a lucky break."

He used his knuckles to knock gently on the side of her head. "Because of a pattern your giant brain figured out. Doesn't matter what got it thinking in that direction."

She kissed him. "Thank you. I know I've been a mess. Everything I've learned about interacting with people seems to have flown out the window over the last few hours. I haven't made many friends here."

He grinned at her—that smile that had her heart stuttering in her chest. "Eh, you're not here to make friends. Everyone's tension level is high. Or maybe everyone's interaction skills have flown out a window."

Penelope's interpersonal skills seemed to be working fine. Bree knew not to say anything. She was tired, stressed and not completely rational.

But damn it, that woman should not look so beautiful. And definitely should not be standing so close to Tanner every time Bree turned around.

"Is everyone else ready to go?" she asked. "I'm ready on my end with the equipment I need. But we'll need to move pretty quickly once I begin to triangulate."

"Yes. There's a solid plan in place. You'll ride with me and Whitaker. Penelope will follow with Leon and a couple other officers."

"We'll have to find the place and be ready and set up by the time he transmits again. Unless for some reason we get extremely lucky, and he's extremely sloppy, the info we get from this first transmission will only lead us part of the way."

Damn it. Why hadn't she figured out a way to bypass whatever rerouting system the killer would use? That would've been a better use of her time rather than hunting for some possible other mistake like Penelope wanted.

"Whatever it is you're thinking—stop," Tanner pulled her close to him one last time. "No focusing on all the things you could've/should've/

would've done. You did the best you could with the info you had."

The time began to beep, signaling the upcoming transmission.

"I hope so. Because we're out of time."

Chapter Eight

It was one of the victim's calmer moments, which didn't necessarily make it any easier to watch. Tanner was afraid she was giving up hope. Everyone was.

Bree's plan needed to work more than ever.

The footage was nearly a minute long this time and the entire room's attention darted back and forth between Bree and the woman on the screen. Once the screen flicked to black and the transmission was over, everyone's attention turned completely to Bree.

She finally looked up. "I got it." She rattled off an address and street name.

"Are you sure?" Penelope asked.

"Yes. That's where this transmission was routed from. Why?"

"If I'm not mistaken that's a residential area. We're going to have to get a warrant," Penelope said.

Jeremy was already at his computer. "Address

belongs to a Patricia Webster. She's actually retired and lives in Tampa. But her twenty-two-year-old son, Elliot Webster, currently resides at Mom's house."

Penelope started rattling off orders. "Leon, I need you to get me a warrant for this address. Karen, get some local uniforms out there until we arrive. Tell them not to engage, but to check for anything that would give them probable cause to enter. Jeremy, I need to know everything there is to know about Elliot Webster by the time we roll up at his house."

Everyone burst into movement.

Tanner looked over at Bree. She was walking toward him, holding a laptop in front of her, typing on the keyboard with one hand.

"You ready to go?" he asked.

She nodded, still typing. "I'm gathering info on Elliot Webster. In case Jeremy…misses any."

Meaning, in case the legal channels Jeremy was required to go through didn't bring up all the information. But Tanner wasn't going to give her a hard time about how she was getting her info right now. This wasn't his case, and a woman's life was at stake.

"Bree," Penelope called out. "We've got nearly the entire four hours until the transmission you need comes around, right?"

Bree looked up from her computer. "Yes, but

I've got to find the computer being used as the conduit before that time. It could be anywhere in or near that address."

"Then let's roll," the woman said. "We've got a judge who's been kept abreast of the case. Getting the warrant should be fast."

Bree was still working at her computer when Tanner tucked her into the car and Whitaker drove toward the address she'd given them, following behind Penelope and her crew.

Bree read from her computer. "It looks like Elliot Webster is an engineering student at UT Dallas. High GPA. Never been arrested or in any trouble at all."

"Anything in the unofficial version?" Tanner asked.

"Not so far. Some clubs at school, a couple of part-time jobs."

"Where at?" Tanner turned to look at her in the back seat.

"Pizza delivery a couple of years ago and one of those giant home improvement stores for the last eighteen months."

"Good place to get low-density polyethylene and any other materials needed to build your very own coffin-sized human aquarium," Whitaker muttered.

"Is this house we're going to anywhere near

where the first two victims were found?" Tanner asked.

"Not at all. I'm as surprised as Penelope that this was where the killer was operating. It's an older neighborhood. Not very upscale, but pretty quiet."

"This probably isn't where the killer is operating," Bree said. "He's just rerouting through his system here."

Tanner rubbed his eyes. "Why would he do that at his own house?"

"That's a good point." Bree's fingers began clicking on the keyboard again. "Elliot Webster could just be a patsy, and someone is using his house while he's not aware. But it's also possible that Webster is the killer and he never thought anyone would figure out his pattern and break his little code."

When they pulled up in front of the house, Tanner understood why Penelope had been so surprised at the address. It was a nice neighborhood—small houses with well-manicured lawns. The type that had Neighborhood Watches and little old ladies peeking out their windows to see what was happening with their neighbors.

Not the type of place to easily get kidnap victims in and out of without being seen.

They parked and Penelope immediately knocked on the front door to make sure no one was around. While they waited for the search warrant since there was no one in the home in immediate danger, the team spread out, looking around the yard and questioning the neighbors. Bree and Jeremy continued to dig for info on Elliot Webster, including known associates.

Less than thirty minutes later they got word the warrant had been approved.

"Let's move in," Penelope said. "You want to come, Tanner?"

He looked over at Bree.

"Go ahead," she said. "You'll do more good in there than out here. I'm going to stay and see what else I can dig up on Elliot."

Penelope handed him a Kevlar vest and began strapping on her own. "What exactly are we looking for in there, Bree?"

"Anything computer related. Try not to touch it if possible. He might have it rigged to notify him if someone messes with it."

Penelope nodded and moved quickly to the front door. Tanner joined Whitaker and they jogged up the front porch steps together.

"Leon and I will swing around to the right," Penelope said. "Whit and Tanner, you head to the left. Everybody stay sharp. I know we don't expect trouble here, but that doesn't mean we won't find it."

She banged on the door. "This is the Dallas police. We have a search warrant for this property and need you to open the door."

Nobody answered. Penelope knocked and identified herself one more time. Everyone had their weapons raised as Leon kicked in the door with as little damage as possible a few seconds later.

Inside, Tanner and Whitaker swung to the left as instructed, checking each room and making sure no one was hiding anywhere. Penelope and Leon did the same on the other side of the house and they eventually met up back in the kitchen.

"We're clear," Whitaker said. "Nobody in the east side of the house."

Penelope and Leon nodded. "Nobody on our side either."

The all holstered their weapons. Now the search began.

"What sort of computer are we looking for?" Whitaker walked around the living room. "Laptop? Desktop?"

Tanner shrugged. "She didn't specify, so keep an eye out for either."

Thirty minutes into searching the house and there was no computer showing up anywhere. Tanner had double-checked all the rooms in the small house himself. They'd *all* double-checked.

"What kind of engineering student doesn't have a computer at his house?" Whitaker asked.

The kind trying to hide a murder.

All four of them made their way back to Elliot's room, the master bedroom. The room was neat, bed made. Different posters hung on the walls—some constellations, an Escher print and a shot of Kate Upton, the famous *Sports Illustrated* swimsuit model. Tanner took a look in the walkin closet again. Small, but nothing suspicious in there either.

It was all just vastly ordinary.

"Nothing about this screams *serial killer*," Tanner said. "And yet…"

"There's something about this room that's just off," Whitaker muttered.

"Exactly. Too perfect, right? Staged to look like how a college student's room should appear." Tanner studied the poster of the beautiful woman in the bikini and where it was situated on the wall. Definitely not where a college kid would put it. "It has to be staged. The Kate Upton poster gives it away."

Whitaker crouched near the bed and whistled through his teeth. "I think you're right."

Penelope came farther into the room behind them, staring at the poster. "Why does this give anything away? What are you seeing that I'm not?"

Whitaker smiled ruefully. "You'll have to lie down on the bed to understand what we mean."

She raised an eyebrow. "That's creepy, Whit. You've gotten weird since you moved to Colorado."

He chuckled. "I know. Just do it."

Penelope lay down, looking ready to jump back up any second. "Okay, I'm down here. What?"

Tanner stepped out of the way so that Penelope had a clearer view of the wall where the posters hung. "What do you see on the walls?"

"The bookshelf is blocking Size DD over there. All I can see are the constellation posters."

"Exactly." Tanner crossed his arms over his chest. "No twenty-two-year-old male would hang that poster of Kate Upton where it couldn't be seen from the bed."

Penelope jumped up from the bed with a shudder. "Okay. But what does it mean?"

Tanner spun around the room again slowly. "It means Elliot Webster is trying to make his mom and anyone else who might visit think that everything is normal with him at first glance. Which means he has some other place that he considers his personal space and feels more comfortable than this room."

"Then why did Bree's calculations lead us here?" Penelope asked. "If this isn't where he spends his time—and obviously isn't where he has his computer—why are we here?"

Tanner shook his head. "I don't know. Maybe

we need to bring her in to look around. See if she sees anything we don't."

They searched through the books and CDs on the shelves but found nothing of interest. The dresser drawers produced clothes, but nothing suspicious.

The walk-in closet was as organized as the bedroom and just as innocuous. A few shirts and pants hanging in the small space. Shoes scattered along the ground. A couple boxes filled with some useless junk—more books, some camping gear, sleeping bags.

Nothing that helped them in any way.

Penelope let out a frustrated sigh. "I don't see anything in here. Grab some of his shoes. We'll take them back to the lab and see if they can find traces of anything, since he's obviously not holding a woman in this house."

Tanner grabbed a pair of well-worn tennis shoes closest to the door and decided to add the hiking boots that sat in the back corner.

One came easily; the other seemed to be stuck to the floor. He tugged hard on it and watched in disbelief as the back panel of the closet clicked open.

His weapon was in his hand in less than a second.

"Guys!" he called, keeping his Glock pointed at the open space in front of him. "There's some sort of secret room behind this wall. I pulled on a shoe and this door cracked open."

There was some sort of secret room behind the closet. No wonder the damned thing seemed so small.

Penelope and Whitaker both rushed back into the closet behind him.

Whitaker cursed when he saw the open panel. "Are you kidding me?"

Tanner tilted his head toward the doorway. "Cover me. I'm going in."

Whitaker moved into place, drawing his weapon and holding the door open. Tanner moved slowly through the opening, ducking since it was only about half the size of a normal door, his own Glock pointed in front of him.

It didn't take long to realize the small room, about half the size of the closet, since that was exactly what it was, didn't have any people in it. There was nowhere to hide anything in here.

But there were definitely computers. A dozen of them. A comfy chair. A well-worn desk.

This was Elliot's personal space.

"It's clear. But we need to get Bree and Jeremy in here right away. We've definitely found our link to the killer."

Chapter Nine

Once the room was deemed secure, Penelope brought Jeremy in. He was typing on the main computer system sitting on the desk. Whitaker, Tanner and Penelope were hanging farther back, staying out of Jeremy's way.

"We need to get Bree in here," Tanner said. "You heard what she said about how the killer might set up the computer system to warn him."

Penelope shook her head. "Not yet. We let Jeremy work. He knows what he's doing. No offense, but your girlfriend is a civilian. She may know computers, but she's not a forensic expert. Plus, she couldn't even remember my name."

"She got us here, didn't she?" Tanner knew how hard it could be trusting someone outside of your own department. But if it wasn't for Bree, they'd all still be sitting watching a woman drown drop by drop.

And despite any names she might have forgotten, Bree was the genius when it came to computers.

"Penelope, let her observe," Whitaker said. "Tanner's right. She got us here. She may see something nobody else does."

Penelope shrugged and turned back to Jeremy. "Fine. But she doesn't touch anything unless she's given the go-ahead by Jeremy."

Jeremy gave a smug little nod, but Tanner didn't call him on it. They were running against a clock, and egos weren't important.

He climbed back out of the secret room and made his way outside. Bree was leaning against the car, laptop in hand, when he got to her.

"This isn't it, is it?" she asked, looking around. "This neighborhood is too busy. There's no way he could have gotten her in here without anybody noticing."

"The house is empty. No sign of the victim or the killer. But it's definitely the right place. We found some sort of secret closet with all sorts of computers."

Her big green eyes got even bigger. "Can I come in? If I have access to his system, I'm sure I can master a backdoor entry and trace where the actual transmissions are coming from. We don't even have to wait for him to make a move."

She was already heading toward the house. He quickly caught up with her. "Freckles, listen, Jeremy gets a crack at it first. This is the Dallas PD's case."

The sour look on her face told him everything he needed to know about her feelings on that subject.

"It is his job and he wants a chance to get some of the credit," he continued.

She rolled her eyes. "I don't care about credit. This is not my job. This is about saving someone's life."

He took her hand in his and they walked up the steps together. "Just see what you can see, but don't take over."

When they got to the secret room, it was just Penelope and Jeremy. Whitaker was helping the other officers search the house more thoroughly.

Bree didn't say anything, but her lips were tight as she watched Jeremy work over his shoulder. Tanner was amazed that Bree was able to keep silent for ten whole minutes. She shifted and he thought she was about to make a suggestion to the other man, but instead she began looking around the room.

"What?" Tanner whispered.

"That's not the right system." Her eyes were darting rapidly to the different computers lying everywhere, at least a dozen. The main one sitting at the desk Jeremy was working on, two other desktop systems on either side and eight or nine different laptops, ranging from top-of-the-line to not much more than paperweights.

"Are you sure? Maybe Jeremy is just missing something?" he whispered as softly as he could.

It wasn't soft enough.

"Hello...sitting right here, you know." Jeremy turned and looked at Bree. "Fine, what am I missing?"

She didn't look at him, just kept studying the computers on the shelves around her.

"Nothing," she finally said. "You're doing everything right. That computer is a dummy system, that's why you can't find what we need. The real system is one of these."

Jeremy turned back to the computer he'd been working on. "Are you kidding me? This system would be a hacker's dream. Why would he not use it?"

Now Bree turned and looked at Jeremy, then at the computer system. "Actually, that's a very good point. Why set that one up as the obvious culprit, unless he *wanted* someone to use it?"

Bree crossed over to Jeremy. Tanner expected her to demand he get out of the way so she could sit down, but instead she pulled the CPU out and turned it so she could see it.

Then muttered a curse.

"What?" Tanner asked.

"Too many wires." She started following the large grouping of wires down past the desk, crawling along the floor to follow them to where they disappeared into a small fuse box.

She cursed again, and Tanner knew they were in trouble. "Freckles, what?"

She ignored him. "Jeremy, open a command prompt window and see if there's a date."

"Why?"

"Just do it!" Bree roared.

"Fine. Okay." Jeremy's fingers clicked on the keyboard. "Okay, I've got it here and…oh, damn."

"Is it a countdown?"

Jeremy nodded, staring at the screen. "Yes. God, Bree, it's counting down from 5, 4, 3, 2…"

Bree dived away from the fuse box as, not a split second later, it exploded all around them, with an ear-piercing squeal and a ball of flames. It knocked out the power, leaving the closet in darkness. Jeremy yelled out, his chair making a huge crash.

"Bree! Jeremy!" Tanner could barely make out anything in the dark, except for the fire that was beginning to climb along the walls.

"I'm okay," she called.

"Jeremy?" Penelope called out.

"I'm alive." The man's voice was tight with pain. "Burned. The computer is toast."

Tanner found Bree's hand and started pulling her toward the door. "We've all got to get out of here."

"Boss," Whitaker called from the doorway.

"The whole house is on fire. Every fuse box and outlet in the place just lit up."

"Get everybody out," Penelope called. "Take anything you can that might help us."

Bree pulled her hand from Tanner's. "I've got to find the killer's operating system. It's one of these other computers."

She turned on the flashlight on her phone to give more light and began looking.

"Bree, we don't have time for this. That fire is going to reach the door and block our way out in just a couple of minutes."

He pulled at her arm, but she yanked it back.

"He knows we're onto him now. That was his fail-safe. He may already have an alarm that lets him know we infiltrated his house. But if not, he'll definitely know once he tries to broadcast again. He'll shut it down. We'll lose him."

Jeremy struggled over beside her, holding his arm and chest at an awkward angle.

"She's right. This is our only chance." He shone his flashlight also. "Probably the Xeon, with the CoreMC, right? It's the most powerful."

"Jeremy, Tanner," Penelope yelled. "Just grab them all, and we'll sort it out later. That fire is getting higher."

Tanner started grabbing the nearest computer. Penelope was right—they just needed to get the computers out. But it jerked a few inches before it wouldn't move anymore. Frowning, he put that one down and tried a different one, with the same result.

He let out a curse. "They're chained. We can't take them with us."

"Everybody out. Now!" Penelope yelled.

"We've got time to try *one*," Jeremy said. "Bree is right. This is our only chance to save this woman's life."

"That one," Bree said, pointing to the one in the lower corner.

"Are you crazy?" Jeremy yelled. "That thing barely looks more powerful than an Atari 2600."

Bree was already opening it. "The Holy Grail is never the jewel-studded goblet. It's the most plain."

The smoke was getting thicker in the room. They had maybe a minute left before they wouldn't be able to breathe.

"This is it!" Bree was already typing, bypassing the manual operating system.

"Freckles, we are running out of time."

She didn't stop typing. "I just need to see the code. I can memorize it. Two minutes."

Tanner looked around the room at the growing fire. "You've got half that."

He turned to the others. "Penelope, get Jeremy out of here. There's nothing more you two can do. I'll get Bree out."

"This is not worth you two dying," the other woman responded. "We'll find another way."

"Get your men out. I'll get Bree out. I'm not going to let anything happen to her."

Bree wasn't saying anything. Her eyes were riveted to the screen as line after line of computer code built in front of her. He didn't try to interrupt. He'd only seen this one other time, when she'd been building the system she needed in order to take down Michael Jeter and the Organization.

She considered it a flaw, the fact that her brain was so much like a computer, able to process data but not so great with emotions. Right now, that computer-type brain was going to save a life.

He stayed at her back, watching the fire, giving her as much time as they could possibly spare to get as much info as she could. It wasn't until the door was about to collapse in on itself that he finally turned and grabbed her. "Time's up. I gave you as long as possible."

She didn't argue, didn't say anything. Just slipped her hand in his and let him lead her out the door.

But once outside of the closet they weren't any safer. They both pulled their jackets over their noses and mouths to try to block the smoke, not that that did much good.

Finding the front door was going to be a bitch. Tanner started leading her as best he could.

"Dempsey! Bree!" Whitaker yelled out from across the room. "Call out!"

"Here!" Tanner returned.

A second later a blast from a fire extinguisher shot in their direction. Whitaker was making a path for them.

They both ran, passing Whitaker, who then turned and followed them out the door.

Tanner could hear the sound of sirens getting closer over his own labored breathing as he and Bree stumbled toward the car.

"Is she okay?" Whitaker got out between harsh breaths of his own.

"Computer," Tanner said. "She needs her computer."

Tanner straightened and helped Bree make it to the car, as Whitaker was getting her laptop out for her. She collapsed, sitting cross-legged on the front lawn, and began typing at a frantic pace. Tanner stood guard over her and let her work. Letting her get the code out now, while it was still fresh in her brain was critical.

Ten minutes later Penelope walked over. Bree was still typing at a frantic pace. "You guys okay?"

"Yeah. Just give her a chance to work."

"Did she get hurt? Her nose is bleeding."

Tanner had been watching that drop of blood leak slowly from Bree's nose for the last five minutes. There was nothing more he wanted to do than wipe it away but knew it wasn't a priority. "Yeah, she's taxing her brain pretty hard."

"What exactly is she doing?"

"She has a unique gift in how she sees and remembers computer coding. Almost a photographic memory. She's re-creating what she can remember and will extrapolate the rest from what she finds."

Jeremy walked up beside Penelope. "Damn. I've heard of stuff like this, but never actually seen it."

Tanner shrugged. "Bree is the best on the planet. She said we've got to catch this guy before the next transmission goes live or else he'll be clued in that we are onto him. He may already be clued in."

Penelope shot them a worried glance. "That's less than thirty minutes. Do you have any idea how long this is going to take her?"

"No. But I do know she's aware of the time crunch and is doing the best she can."

"We won't make the mistake of doubting her again," Penelope said. "Let us know if there's anything we can do to help."

"Just be ready to move when she is."

BREE FELT LIKE she was coming out of a dream.

But a dream where she had been held down and kicked in the head multiple times.

"I'm done." Her voice sounded much weaker than she had intended it to, reminding her of the weeks after she'd been strangled, when her voice wouldn't work no matter how hard she tried to make it.

She cleared her throat and tried again. "I'm done." Much better. "The program I built is tracing his and we should have a location any minute now."

She tried to stand up but dizziness immediately assaulted her.

"Whoa, there." Tanner's arm wrapped around her, and a water bottle was lifted to her mouth. She gratefully drank, then didn't argue when Tanner forced a candy bar up to her lips.

"Did everybody make it out of the fire okay?"

It felt so good to rest against Tanner's chest as he pulled her against him. "Yes. You, me and Whitaker were the last ones out. Bastard set the whole house to burn."

"We're going to catch him. What I was able to remember was more than enough."

He kissed her forehead. "You're spooky scary when that giant brain of yours gets going. Sexiest thing I've ever seen."

Now that was what she wanted to hear. "Then

how about we catch this guy and you take me to the hotel and show me exactly how sexy you think it is."

"That would be my pleasure."

Bree's computer chirped. She pushed away from Tanner, ignoring the dizziness.

"That's it. We've got him." She turned the computer toward Tanner. "This general area. It will get more specific as we get closer."

Tanner took the computer and showed it to the blonde perfect lady. Bree didn't even try to remember her name this time.

The blonde nodded and called out to everyone. "Warehouse district on the south side. Let's move!"

Tanner helped Bree back into the car. She was having a hard time keeping her eyes open, much less focusing. Whitaker climbed into the back seat and Tanner reached over from the driver's seat and grabbed her hand, bringing it up to his lips. "I know you're tired. Hang with us just a few more minutes."

She nodded. But the next thing she knew, Tanner was squeezing her hand and shaking her awake.

"We're closer, freckles. I need you to give me as much detail about the location as possible."

Bree forced herself to focus, clicking the keys to get the information they needed. The characters were blurry and she had to blink multiple times to get them clear. Finally, she read him an address. Whitaker immediately repeated it over his phone to the other cars.

"My program isn't running anymore, so that should be the final address," she said.

"This place makes a hell of a lot more sense than a residential neighborhood," Whitaker responded. "Much more isolated, much easier to move a kidnap victim or body."

Bree nodded. It was all she could do to keep her eyes open. "You guys have to be careful. At the very least he knows somebody found his secret room."

"But he doesn't know you figured out what computer he was using," Tanner said.

"That's true. He'll probably still want to shut everything down, but maybe he thinks he has more time and won't do anything drastic."

Like kill the victim outright.

Bree couldn't stand the thought that they might lose her this close to saving her life.

Five minutes later they were pulling up in front of what looked to be an abandoned warehouse. Bree tried to focus but found herself continuously closing her eyes.

"You rest now." Tanner kissed her forehead. "You've done your part. Let them do theirs."

"You're not going in?" The thought did not make her sad at all.

"I'll do whatever they need me to, but this is Penelope's call."

Penelope. The blonde. Bree's eyes drifted closed, a scowl on her lips at the other woman's name.

"Is she out?" Whitaker asked as he opened the door.

Tanner got out too. "Yes. Her body is done."

They jogged over to the other car parked a few yards from them.

"SWAT wants us to wait," Penelope said. "But they are twenty minutes out. We definitely don't have that kind of time."

"Bree says the guy definitely knows we're onto him. He might not know we're closing in on him now, but he's going to be much more wary," Tanner told them.

"Even more reason to move in now." Penelope turned to the uniformed officer who had followed them from the house. "Kelly, you stay here. Keep an eye on Bree and make sure our perp doesn't get away if he comes running out the front door."

Young officer Kelly nodded. "Yes, ma'am."

Penelope looked over at Tanner and he gave her

a nod. Knowing someone had Bree's back freed him up to go inside.

Penelope turned to them. "Okay, people, we're going in there blind, so be careful. Leon and I will take the front door. Whit, you and Tanner take the back."

They didn't waste any time. Tanner and Whitaker made their way around the back of the building, opening a rusty door as quietly as possible. As soon as they were inside, they realized there hadn't really been any need to be quiet. Someone was screaming their head off so loudly, hearing anything was damn near impossible.

"Please! The water! Please, he turned it up!"

Tanner and Whitaker both darted in the direction of the voice. They both knew it could be a trap, but they weren't going to leave a woman to die.

Thankfully she kept screaming, leading them deeper into the warehouse, where four walls had been set up to give the appearance of a small room. There wasn't even a proper door.

This was where the footage had come from.

As Tanner and Whitaker stormed inside the facade, the woman let out a terrified shriek garbled by the water that was now about to cover her face. There was no sign of the killer anywhere, and nowhere he could hide.

Tanner kneeled down and reached under the woman's head to lift her farther out of the water.

"There's a man," she said, struggling to get in air. "I—I—"

Tanner nodded. "Shh. Just focus on breathing. We'll catch the guy who put you in here."

Whitaker already had his phone out and on speaker. "Penelope, we've got the victim alive, but there's no sign of the kidnapper."

"We just spotted him coming out of the Northwest corner of the building." Penelope's voice was labored, obviously running. "Stay with the victim. Leon and I will catch him. Backup is en route."

Whitaker turned to Tanner, taking in the situation. "Let me get the water turned off and find something for us to bail out some of it, before it covers her face."

They wouldn't be able to get her out of her shackles until more specialized help arrived. All they could do was keep her alive until then. Whitaker shut off the hose that was raining down the water then found an empty cup. It wasn't much, but now that water wasn't filling the box, it was enough for them to keep the woman from drowning.

They both tried to talk soothingly to her as they got out as much water as they could. Tanner didn't recognize her as anyone famous, but he didn't live around here. His best guess was that she was in her thirties. She had reddish-blond hair and, like Shelby and Kelly Quinn, was about five foot three and one hundred pounds.

Tanner reached down into the water and grabbed the woman's hand, both to offer comfort and to stop her from pulling at the restraints. "Hey, what's your name?"

"Jean Adams," she finally managed to get out.

"You're doing so great, Jean, okay? We're not going to leave you. Someone is going to be with you every second until they get you out of here, okay?"

She nodded, her breathing already a little bit steadier.

Tanner looked over at Whitaker and raised an eyebrow. Whitaker shook his head and shrugged. Evidently Jean Adams wasn't a celebrity to him either.

Whitaker continued to bail out water and Tanner held Jean's hand, talking to her about almost-nonsensical things. He didn't want to question her about anything important or difficult and cause her to get upset again. It wasn't long before the other members of the Dallas PD were coming through the door.

But nothing was as good as the text Whitaker

got just a few minutes later from Penelope. He turned it around so Tanner could read it himself.

Fleeing suspect apprehended and in custody.

It was over.

Chapter Ten

Six hours after she'd fallen asleep in an exhausted heap in the car, Bree was about to fade into oblivion again. But this time it was because Tanner was currently standing behind her in the large hotel shower and was washing her hair.

"You fading on me again, freckles?"

"Can you blame me this time?" She couldn't stop her little moan as he rubbed his fingers more deeply into her scalp.

He reached down and kissed her shoulder. "I didn't blame you last time. You needed it. We caught Elliot Webster because of you."

She shrugged. "It was a team effort. But yeah, mostly me."

He chuckled and kissed her shoulder again.

"Do you think Jean is going to be okay?" she asked.

Tanner pulled her back under the spray of the water. "Physically, yes. We got to her before any real damage could be done by the water. She's at the hospital, mostly for observation."

"But emotionally?"

He cupped his hand over her forehead so no soap would run into her eyes and tilted her head back. "It's hard to know exactly what sort of emotional scars this leaves on a person. I daresay she might not take a bath for the rest of her life."

Bree wouldn't blame her. "But she's alive—that's the most important thing."

"Absolutely. Always the most important thing."

They finished rinsing and stepped out of the shower.

She peeked over at him as she dried off her face, trying not to stare at his abs. Was it ridiculous that she still couldn't get enough of looking at his body even after all these months? She finally tore her eyes away. "Did Elliot Webster admit to killing Whitaker's friend and the other lady?"

Tanner dried off that sexy chest, then wrapped his towel low around his hips. "Not that I've heard. I'm sure Whitaker will keep us posted, but as far as I know, Elliot hasn't talked at all."

"I guess that doesn't serve his best interests to admit to multiple murders."

"Speaking of multiple murders, you going to be okay with the whole Jeter situation?" Tanner leaned back against the vanity counter and grabbed both edges of her towel, pulling her up against him.

She sighed and leaned against him. "Honestly, I'm just trying not to think about it. I'm definitely relieved about not having to testify. And I had never really thought about his sentencing. But I don't guess I can blame him for working out a deal where he can't get the death penalty. And I can't blame the prosecuting attorneys for wanting to get this over with as quickly and inexpensively as possible."

"But?"

She shrugged. "I guess it just all seems too easy."

"Sometimes people take the easy way out when they don't have better options."

"Yeah, I know. But I think maybe I mean it was too easy for *me*."

Tanner pulled her in closer to his chest and she breathed in the warm, wet, male scent of him. "Nothing about the situation with Jeter has ever been easy for you."

"Maybe it was that I had accepted that I was going to have to face him when I testify, even though I was scared. I was finally going to look him in the eye and make people understand what a monster he is, not only for the terrorist stuff he did, but for what he did to me. Although, I guess in the greater scheme of things that's really not what's important."

His fingers came up to comb gently through her wet hair. "He had all the power when you were a child. He did unspeakable things to you— you've got the physical and mental scars to prove it. It's more than understandable to want to finally take some of that power back. To look him in the eye and make him know that he holds nothing over you now."

"Yes." All that. Tanner understood. He always understood, even when she didn't.

"I'm sorry you don't get to have that. You deserve it."

"No. The important thing is that Jeter is going to jail for the rest of his life. He's not going to have control over anything, especially me." She squeezed him again, realizing how much she meant it.

They walked into the bedroom together. Bree smothered a yawn. She didn't want Tanner to think she was too tired to utilize the lovely-looking king-size bed here in the hotel. He got so overprotective when she did stuff like pass out from exhaustion.

But at least he was watching her as she dropped the towel to the ground and slipped under the sheets naked. "So, I guess our part is done here since Elliot is in custody."

"Yeah, Penelope will take over now."

"Perfect Penelope." Bree knew she was sulking, being ridiculous, but couldn't help it. She didn't even like to hear the woman's name.

Tanner climbed in bed beside her. "Not perfect, but I was pretty impressed with how she's handled this entire investigation. It's a lot of pressure and she seemed to manage her people pretty well."

"And she also happens to be blonde and gorgeous."

"Why, Miss Daniels, I do believe you sound a little bit jealous."

"What could there possibly be to be jealous of? The woman is smart, has a career in law enforcement, could be mistaken for a supermodel and is attracted to you."

Before she even knew what was happening, Bree found herself rolled over and tucked under Tanner's big, naked body.

"There's only one person I'm interested in, and she very fortunately happens to be in this bed with me."

Bree's eyes drifted closed, her breath hissing slowly out of her as his mouth found her neck and began nibbling down the side of it. This man had taught her everything she knew about pleasure. Everything she knew about trust. Everything she knew about love.

"I'm sorry for what I said at the ranch." Before they made love again she wanted to make sure the air was cleared from that. "I know I said something wrong and it hurt you. I'm sorry."

Tanner shifted his weight onto his elbows and looked down into her eyes. "We've got some stuff to work out, that's for sure. Things we need to sit down and talk honestly about—plans. What we both want now, and what we both want going into the future."

"I want *you*."

That handsome face broke into a grin. "Good, because I want you too. And as long as were committed to each other—"

"—and no blonde, gorgeous detectives—"

He kissed her. "—that's all that we need to know for sure right now."

"Then kiss me, Captain Hot Lips, and let's not let this gorgeous hotel suite go to waste."

"Oh, I'm going to do a lot more than kiss you."

All she could do was hold on to him as he did.

A LOUD BANGING on the hotel door jerked Tanner completely awake. He immediately reached for his Glock on the bedside table, quickly getting his bearings.

Bree rolled over in the bed, muttering, "Want to sleep."

The pounding on the door came again. Tanner

slipped on his boxers and glanced at his phone. It was 4:30 a.m. He cursed when he saw he'd missed a dozen messages from Whitaker, since his phone had been on silent so Bree could get some sleep.

Sure enough when he looked out the hotel door security hole, there was Whitaker.

Tanner opened the door. "You do know it's four thirty in the morning, right?"

Whitaker didn't crack a smile. "We need you and Bree back at the station right away. We've got a situation."

Tanner left the door open for Whitaker to enter and grabbed his jeans from the bathroom, slipping them on. "Are you sure she has to come with us? She's still pretty wiped from yesterday."

Whitaker shook his head grimly. "Yes, unfortunately we need her more than we even need you. We just received more footage."

Shock shot through Tanner's body. "What? I don't understand. Could it have been previously recorded?"

Whitaker shrugged. "It doesn't look like it, but let's hope so."

"Did Elliot Webster have a second victim somewhere? A partner?"

"We're trying to figure out exactly what is going on. Jeremy is still in the hospital because of his burns, and Penelope is hesitant to bring an unknown person into the case at this point. So Bree is the best option."

"What's going on?" Bree said from the bed, sitting up and holding the sheet pulled up to her body.

"I'll wait outside." Whitaker immediately turned and walked out the door.

Tanner walked over to the bed. "We've got a problem, freckles. More footage arrived at the station. With Jeremy at the hospital they need you to authenticate it and let us know what is going on—whether it's old or new."

She stretched like a sleepy kitten, then rubbed her eyes. He should've let her sleep last night instead of keeping them both awake half the night. But neither of them had seemed to be able to get enough of each other. It was like both of them wanted to resolidify whatever parts had become shaky over the last few days.

And they had. Their bond was 100 percent secure. They still needed to work out the details about what their always was going to look like, but that was all it was: details. That ring was still in his jacket pocket. As soon as the time was right he was going to slip it on her finger.

He tucked a strand of her brown hair behind her ear. "You go hop in the shower. I'll get us some coffee. It's time to go back to work."

Chapter Eleven

There was a skeleton crew working at command central when they got there. Penelope gave them both a solemn nod. "Thank you for coming in again. We are a little bit shaken up by this footage and just want to know what we're dealing with."

Bree sat down and pulled up the footage. Tanner hated to see the pinched look back in her eyes.

None of them spoke as they watched twenty-four seconds of what looked to be Jean Adams back in that damned water coffin. She wasn't talking, wasn't crying, but did seem to be lying there muttering something. With the voice modulator it was impossible to make out her words.

When the footage shut off, they all looked over at Bree.

She shook her head, looking confused. "I need a few minutes to see what I can figure out."

Tanner squeezed her shoulder.

"Do you mind playing it again, or will that disrupt what you're doing?" Penelope asked her.

"No, I'll play it again." Bree sat down to work as the footage came back up on the screen.

"Okay," Penelope said. "What can we see? Anything. Different, same."

"The water is higher," Tanner said. "By at least a couple of inches from the last footage we received."

Everybody looked closer.

"He's right," Whitaker said. "But the water is still dripping at the same rate. Not gushing down like it was when we found Jean."

Tanner rubbed his eyes, trying to make sense of this. The footage had to be from earlier in the day, prerecorded. They watched the footage again.

"Did we ever figure out if Jean is someone we should know?" Tanner asked. "Why Elliot was using a voice modulator and not ever showing her face?"

Penelope shook her head. "Nothing so far."

"You guys," Bree called out. "I've got something."

As soon as Tanner saw her face—and the worry in those beautiful green eyes—he knew they were in trouble.

"What?"

Bree looked like she wasn't going to be able to get the words out.

"Just say it," Penelope told her. "Any information is better than not knowing what's in front of us at all."

Bree shook her head. "There's bad news, and worse news. This footage is definitely not on a loop. It wasn't something Elliot prerecorded to send out later."

They all muttered curses.

Bree turned to Penelope. "Did the crime lab dismantle the camera that had been used to record at the crime scene?"

Penelope nodded. "Yes, in order to take it in as evidence it was removed from the wall. But there are plenty of pictures of exactly where it hung."

"So since there was going to be no more footage being sent, I assume you sent your computer team home."

Penelope nodded again. "Yes. They'd been working nearly forty-eight hours straight. It seemed pointless to keep them around when they had already done their part."

"I understand," Bree said. But she didn't look happy about it.

"So what exactly is your worse news?" Penelope asked.

Bree typed on her keyboard for a few seconds.

"Nobody was here, but the program I uploaded that recorded all the screens captured everything we need. The program everyone was mad at."

Tanner could see Penelope was getting frustrated with Bree for not getting to the point quicker. Bree tended to think that everyone wanted all the details like she always wanted the details.

"Just hit us with the bottom line, freckles."

Bree's green eyes flew to his. "It's been nine hours since you rescued Jean Adams. But at the top of each hour since then there's been another clip that was broadcasted."

"What the hell does that mean?" Penelope asked.

"It means there's another victim," Bree said. "And her water is already past where Jean's was."

Whitaker muttered a curse under his breath.

Bree sat back down at the computer. "I've got to work. We don't have a lot of time."

TANNER MADE SURE Bree had a steaming cup of coffee next to her keyboard, then walked over to Whitaker and Penelope.

"I've called everybody back in," she said. "Hopefully they got enough of a break to be able to look at this with fresh eyes."

"I don't understand." Whitaker scrubbed a hand down his face. "What is this, a copycat? If so, how? How could they have gotten all the details so perfectly in such a short amount of time?"

"They couldn't," Tanner said. "This had to

have been someone working with Elliot from the beginning."

Penelope walked over and poured herself a cup of coffee. "We haven't been looking too deeply into his known associates, but that's where we'll start. I interviewed him briefly, but he wasn't very talkative. He hasn't lawyered up yet, so I figured I'd let him sweat for a little while."

"Now might be a good time to see if the sweating worked," Tanner said.

Penelope nodded. "You guys want to join me?"

Penelope handed Tanner a file as they walked through the main section of the building toward the holding cells. "A refresher course on Elliot. Twenty-two-year-old engineering student. Straight As through high school and college. No priors. No known affiliation with any groups or people that would raise red flags."

Tanner nodded. He remembered this much from what Bree had told them before they'd infiltrated the building. He handed the folder back to Penelope. "You've talked to him. What's your take on him? We all know a file is only going to help so much."

Penelope opened the door and they walked into the observation room. On the other side of the two-way glass sat Elliot Webster.

"Tends to think he's the smartest person in the room," Penelope said. "Hell, he probably is most of the time. I'm sure we're talking Mensa IQ and damned if the kid isn't afraid to let everybody know it."

Tanner studied Elliot through the window. The kid definitely didn't look scared. Bored maybe, but not frightened.

There wasn't too much impressive about him, at least physically. Blondish-brown hair that looked like it needed a cut. Eyes too close together on a face too pointed and angled. He was probably about five foot nine and 160 pounds.

Basically, quite ignorable.

"And he hasn't asked for a lawyer?"

Penelope shook her head. "Nope."

"Definitely a cocky bastard," Whitaker muttered. "Guy does remember that we caught him right smack in the middle of attempted murder, right?"

"I'll be honest." Penelope leaned in closer to stare at him. "I think this is all just part of a game to him, the same as sending the footage. I think he plans to lawyer up, but wants to play us as long as possible."

Tanner nodded. "We can use his own conceit against him. He hasn't asked for a lawyer because he's sure we won't be able to trip him up with our questions. And that may end up being true, but I say we work his own plan against him for as long as possible."

Whitaker looked at Penelope. "Do you mind if Tanner and I try to talk to him? He's met you, but doesn't know who we are at all."

"Be my guest. I'll watch from out here and see if I catch anything from him."

Tanner and Whitaker walked into the room. Elliot straightened up slightly in his chair. "Finally," he muttered.

"We understand you're denying your right to counsel," Whitaker said as he sat down across from Elliot. Tanner remained standing, leaning against the wall.

Elliot raised one eyebrow. "Yeah, that's right. I think I'm doing just fine without one."

Definitely a cocky bastard.

"That's your choice, of course," Whitaker confirmed. "As long as you know you can request one at any time."

Elliot tilted his head to the side. "Plus, you only have a few more hours before you're required to charge me, or let me go."

Cocky bastard who knew the law.

Whitaker nodded. "That's right. And you will be charged, seeing as how we caught you in the act of attempted murder."

Tanner's eyes narrowed. That's what Elliot was waiting on before calling a lawyer—an official charge. But why wait if he knew it was coming?

Tanner decided to see if he could find out what made Elliot tick. He pressed up from against the wall. "We got your videos."

Elliot straightened slightly, for the first time not looking completely bored. "Never doubted you would. Is that how you found me?"

Bingo. That was why he hadn't called his lawyer. He knew once he did he wouldn't get his answers. He wanted to know how he'd gotten caught.

"Yep. Was able to trace them right to you with no problem."

Elliot's eyes narrowed. "I know that's not true."

Tanner raised a brow. "Because you're too smart for us to trace them?"

"In this case, yes. Smarter than you guys, at least."

Whitaker leaned back in his chair and glanced over at Tanner. "I don't know about that. I'm a pretty smart guy. Or at least my mom always says so."

Tanner grinned at him, glad that Whitaker had caught on so quickly. "Me too, you know. I wasn't surprised when we were able to track Elliot here to the warehouse so quickly."

The kid crossed his arms over his chest. "There is no way you two were able to track me."

Time to see what Elliot was willing to spill.

"Maybe we didn't have to track you. Maybe your partner gave you up. Told us who you were and where you'd be."

A smooth smile fell onto Elliot's face. "Is that right?"

Tanner kept his face neutral. "You sure that's not what happened? Do you trust him so much that you're sure he won't betray you even to save his own skin?"

The kid's smile got bigger. "Something like that."

Whitaker looked over at Tanner, eyes narrowed just a little bit. He was thinking the same thing Tanner was. Elliot was way too relaxed in his answers about a partner to be truly concerned that someone might have betrayed him.

Nobody involved with a crime like this would be that secure a partner hadn't flipped on them in order to save their own skin.

Tanner wasn't sure how it was possible with this new footage showing up, but it didn't look like Elliot was working with anyone.

He just continued to sit there, smug, strumming his fingers on the metal table.

Whitaker didn't get flustered. "Okay, you caught us. Not a partner. Maybe you just got sloppy with your encoding. All the VPNs and routers in the world can't hide a mistake if we've got someone just as good as you."

If possible, Elliot just got more superior in his seat. "Yep, I guess that must be how you did it."

Tanner decided to give Elliot a little bit of what he wanted. See if that got a reaction. "Fractal pattern."

When it came down to it, the kid didn't have much of a poker face after all. He sat bone straight in his chair at Tanner's words, realizing for the first time that maybe they *did* have someone just as good as him. "What?"

"You were using a fractal pattern in your transmission, right? Still think we're stupid now, Elliot?"

He was shaking his head. "How did you—"

A knock on the door stopped Tanner from saying anything further. Penelope stuck her head in. "Tanner, can I talk to you for a moment?"

Elliot was still trying to wrap his head around the fact that they'd figured out his precious code. Whitaker gave him a nod and Tanner walked into the observation room.

"What is it? We're just starting to make headway on—" He stopped when he saw Bree standing there.

"I think I've figured it out," she said. "Can I ask Elliot a couple of questions about codes?"

Tanner looked over at Penelope. "Your call."

Penelope gave a slow nod. "Two minutes. Keep it short and remember all of this is being recorded."

Bree nodded and they walked back into the room together. Elliot had regained a little bit of his composure.

"What?" he sneered. "Are you bringing in the pretty good cop to be the yin to your bad cop's yang?"

"No, Elliot," Tanner said smoothly. "You were right before when you said you were smarter than Whitaker and me. I've brought in the person you're not smarter than. The one who figured out your little code. Figured out which computer was yours at your house and got the info she needed before the fire could burn the place to the ground. Figured out how to get you locked up in here now."

Elliot's eyes narrowed on Bree. He was close to her age so didn't make the mistake of discounting her out of hand just because she was young. "Is that so, sexy? Are you smarter than me?"

Bree crossed over to the table before Tanner could stop her. "Matrix grid pattern torus."

Tanner had no idea what she was talking about—it sounded more like she was trying to cast out demons than ask Elliot a question.

But evidently the casting out worked. Every

bit of color drained from Elliot's face. He turned to Whitaker.

"I'd like to call my lawyer now."

Maya Grayson

Elliot didn't even Bree a chance to reply. He turned to Whitaker.

"I'd like to call my lawyer now.

Chapter Twelve

Bree wanted to ask Elliot more about the torus, to get him to admit that was the new pattern even though she was almost positive it was. But Tanner immediately ushered her out of the interrogation as soon as Elliot mentioned a lawyer. Whitaker followed right behind them.

As soon the door closed, Tanner turned to Penelope. "You heard the request for counsel?"

She nodded. "Yes. I'm glad you left right away. We don't want to risk any chance of Elliot getting off on a technicality."

"Besides, Bree got what she needed," Tanner said.

Bree looked at him. "I did? Elliot didn't answer my question."

"You wanted to know if the matrix torus thing meant something to him."

"Yes. But he didn't answer."

Tanner smiled gently at her. "It meant something to him, freckles. Something enough to scare him into calling for his lawyer when nothing else had. So whatever it is you've found? You're on the right track."

She looked around at the three of them. "I don't think you're going to like what I found."

Penelope sighed. "Tell us anyway."

"We have *three* more victims. Jean Adams was only one of four."

Whitaker cursed. "He does have partners. I'm going back in there to talk to him. Get some answers."

Penelope put her hand against the door. "No. Not until he has a chance to call his lawyer."

"It will probably be easier for me to show you everything back in the command room," Bree said. "I think you're going to want to watch all the footage again. Once I figured out the pattern, I certainly did."

"Are you sure there are more victims?" Penelope asked. "And how do you know that there are three more?"

"I found another code," Bree said after Penelope assigned another detective the task of making sure Elliot was able to call his lawyer. They practically ran back toward the command center.

"I thought you had already looked for other codes but hadn't found any," Whitaker said.

Bree nodded. "This one wasn't here yesterday. This new code started once we rescued Jean Adams."

Tanner rubbed his eyes. "I don't understand all this code stuff. Why utilize it?"

"It's complex. But I'm not surprised about this because of Elliot's engineering background."

As soon as they made it back to the command area, Bree walked immediately over to the whiteboard. She drew a large square. She wrote Jean Adams at one corner. Then she took a different color and connected the three remaining corners in a triangle.

"The matrix grid pattern torus is a pattern found all over nature. It's studied in mathematics. Some scientists argue that it will eventually be used to create renewable energy. But for our purposes, it's important because it's a pattern based specifically on the number three."

She was about to go into more about the codes, but Tanner put his hand on her shoulder and rubbed it gently. She needed to get to the main point more quickly.

She closed her eyes and regrouped. Focus just on the victims.

"The voice modulator. That should've been our first clue that there was something going on. Jean Adams isn't famous. Nobody would've recognized her face or voice. But we all might've recognized that we were looking at four different victims on the footage if we could've heard or seen them clearly."

Whitaker nodded. "That makes more sense than anything else we've come up with."

"Yes," Bree said. "Like I said before, the footage never stopped coming in even after you rescued Jean. We just weren't expecting it, so didn't realize it. And the water in the new footage is still rising at the same rate. We're still on the same deadline we were with Jean. The dripping water with all four victims started at the same time."

Tanner looked over at the clock. "So we have what, less than twenty-four hours before these other three victims drown?"

Whitaker nodded. "About that. If you don't take hypothermia into account."

"Tell us what you know about these other three victims," Penelope said.

Bree grimaced. The matrix torus pattern had shown her there were three victims, but it didn't give the sort of details the detective was going to want to know. "The killers all started at the exact same time and have created rooms to look exactly alike. That's how they fooled us with the footage."

Tanner looked around at the screens. "So the pattern helped you distinguish which footage belongs to which victim?"

Bree nodded. "I've already got the footage clips lined up so you can look at them together holistically. Once you understand that it's four different people we're looking at, you can't help but see it."

Bree played the grouped footage for them. She started with the most obvious, and the most heartbreaking: the woman who was crying all the time. They watched it in silence.

"It wasn't that she was upset sometimes," Tanner whispered. "This victim is upset *all* the time."

Bree nodded, then showed them the second grouping of footage—the victim who never tried to communicate with them at all.

"I think maybe she can't see any indication of the camera," Whitaker said after they watched the clips all the way through twice. "Everyone else got more hysterical or louder when they knew the camera clicked on, but not her. Maybe she doesn't even know she's being recorded at all."

The rest of the team was trickling back in and Penelope was briefing them as they did. Everyone was now studying the footage in their proper groups. It at least helped make sense out of the behavior of the women.

Fifteen minutes later Whitaker confirmed that they did in fact have multiple victims when he spotted a tiny tattoo on the foot of the second victim they'd given the name Jane B.

"It's right above her pinkie toe on her left foot," Whitaker pointed out. "I don't know how we missed this before."

"Because we assumed we were looking at the same person," Tanner said. "We weren't comparing them to each other."

Penelope called the chaos to order. "People. I know this is a lot, but we've got to get organized and focused."

Everyone immediately quieted down. Penelope turned to Bree. "Can you track these transmissions the way you did Elliot Webster?"

It was the question Bree had been dreading. "No. The pattern doesn't have anything to do with how they're transmitting, just the order and the length of the clips."

"But they are partners with Elliot, right?" Whitaker asked.

This was a little harder to explain. "I'm not sure *partners* is the right word. Obviously this was planned out together to some degree. They all had to have been using the same schematics. To fool us for this long they each had to build the room with the same dimensions, with the cameras set at the exact same angle and height. They had to choose women whose body types were similar enough that we would mistake them for each other."

"Sounds like partners to me," someone muttered.

Bree shrugged. "Maybe they are. They all obviously agreed to use the matrix torus pattern for which victim is shown in what order and for how long. But they were left to their own devices for the actual encryption and encoding of the footage."

"So, not partners," Tanner said.

Bree rubbed her forehead. "Almost like competitors, but that's not right either."

"Elliot is an engineering student. So maybe not partners or competitors. They're collaborators in an experiment." Penelope said.

"That would make sense." Bree thought back on everything she'd found. "It's twisted, but it's like they all had the same set of instructions and just had to build it to the specifications."

"It's all great to know the why," Leon said. "But how do we stop them? If Bree can't track them, we're basically back to square one. Every hour we're getting footage, and granted this time we know we are looking at three different women, but how do we *find* them?"

Penelope moved everyone over to the conference table. "We start with what info we do have. We need to do a statewide missing persons search. We have a definite MO when it comes to victims. Female, five foot three to five foot four, no more than 110 pounds. That can't be a very big list."

Leon nodded and stood up. "I'm on it."

Penelope turned to Bree. "We have a warrant

for anything Elliot saved online. Whether these guys were partners, colleagues or competitors, they had to have had some sort of interaction with each other."

Bree nodded. Depending on how much Elliot had saved, and what safety defaults he had when he realized his defenses had been triggered, the information they found in his online data storage might or might not be useful. But it was definitely worth a try.

"Absolutely. I'll start searching through it, ghosting and rebuilding as much as possible for any missing data."

"What about us, boss?" Whitaker asked. "What do you want Tanner and me to do?"

"We're going back to see if Elliot's lawyer is here yet. Elliot is the one person who has answers and we've got to get them from him."

Chapter Thirteen

Bree was already starting to sort through the data Elliot had saved to the cloud when Tanner walked over to her five minutes later.

"I'm going with Penelope and Whitaker to interview Elliot again." He kissed the top of her head. "Are you okay? Do you need a break?"

It was impossible not to be concerned about her. Bree was a civilian. Law enforcement wasn't her job. She'd already put in long hours yesterday and that didn't even include the havoc she'd wreaked on her body trying to remember the coding at Elliot's house. It was unfair of them to ask her to continue to work at this pace, but the lives of three women were at stake.

"I'm okay. My mind is starting to readapt to this pace. Jeter used to work me like this." Her fingers never stopped tapping on the keyboard even as she spoke. "Not just me, all of his prodigies. He pushed us hard, way too hard, and then we were punished if we couldn't do it."

Tanner had seen some of the scars on her body from Jeter's punishments. The thought that they were doing the same thing to her now made him physically ill.

He crouched down beside her. "Freckles, look at me."

She did, but just for a second.

He reached up and cupped her cheek with his hand, forcing her to look at him. Her hands stilled on the keyboard. "This is not the same. You can take a break whenever you want to. If you need to go sleep for a couple hours, get up and stretch, hell, go take a shower? All of those are okay and everyone would understand."

She twisted her head and kissed the inside of his palm. "I know that. I can tough it out. I like that, for once, what Jeter did to me is leading to something good, rather than something painful. Like you said, I don't get to take any of my power back in court. Maybe this could be the next best thing."

Any doubt that he'd had—and there really hadn't been any—about whether he wanted to spend the rest of his life with this woman was erased in that moment. "I love you," he said.

Hell, he was already down on one knee, he was halfway tempted to ask her to marry him right now. But that wasn't the story he wanted her telling their grandkids. He would wait until the right time.

"I love you too, hot lips. Now go get some information on Elliot. We've got lives to save."

He kissed her quickly and stood. She was already clicking away on her keyboard again.

Tanner jogged to catch up with Whitaker and Penelope as they headed toward the door.

"Bree okay?" Whitaker asked.

"She's running on empty, but she's strong."

"No doubt about that." Whitaker nodded, then turned to Penelope. "You know Elliot's lawyer is not going to let him talk to us. Even if he's not here yet, he would've given that instruction when they talked on the phone."

Penelope pressed her lips together as she nodded. "We're actually going to do this all off-the-record. Right now I care more about saving those other women's lives than I do about making sure Elliot goes down. We'll deal with the ramifications when we have to."

"What's your plan?" Tanner asked.

"I'm going to get into the room where the interrogation cameras are kept. I can probably buy us a window of ten minutes. Nothing will be recorded in that time. I'm not saying to hurt him—I'm just saying be as persuasive as possible."

Whitaker stopped walking and grabbed Penelope's arm. "Pen. If you get caught, that could mean your badge. At the very least you won't ever be doing detective work again."

She shrugged. "It's a risk I'm willing to take, especially if it means we're not going to watch three women drown in some sick water coffin. That's why I brought you guys rather than anybody else on the team. If I get caught and you two get busted, you're going to get a slap on the wrist and sent back to Colorado. I didn't want to take a chance with anyone else."

Tanner nodded, understanding. He believed in the justice system, but sometimes when your hands were tied, you had to use whatever tools you could reach. They weren't always the best, but they were the only option. "You buy us ten minutes. We'll get as much as we can out of him."

They came to a fork in the hallways.

"Wait for my text, then move as quickly as you can." Penelope took the turn to the left, and he and Whitaker continued down to the interview room.

"I hope this doesn't blow up in our faces," Tanner muttered as they arrived at the outside door.

Whitaker shrugged and opened it. "Penelope has the most to lose. But yeah, I don't want to see Elliot walking free because of a mistrial."

They could see Elliot through the two-way mirror, picking his nails. He definitely looked less confident than when they'd interviewed him before. Bree's words had spooked him.

A few seconds later Whitaker's phone chimed. "That's Penelope. Let's do this."

They walked inside.

"Where's my lawyer?" Elliot asked.

"I'm sure he'll be here any minute." Tanner sat down across from Elliot this time and Whitaker stood up against the wall. "We're not here in any official police capacity."

Tanner took his badge out and slid it across the table.

Elliot studied it for a second. "That says Colorado."

Tanner nodded. "That's right. Whitaker and I both work in the Grand County Sheriff's Department in Colorado. We have no jurisdiction here. We just want to talk person to person before your lawyer gets here. Nothing you say here is going to be admissible in court."

"Look," Whitaker added. "If your partners kill those women, you're going down with them for conspiracy to commit. The only way to save yourself that charge is to tell us who and where they are."

Elliot crossed his arms over his chest. "I don't know."

Tanner put his elbows on the table. "Don't know *who* or don't know *where*?"

"Both, okay? I met them online. I don't know who they are and they don't know who I am. We all agreed to some rules—patterns we all had to follow—and thought it would be a cool game."

Whitaker took a step closer. "You thought it would be a *cool game* to drown women slowly in a coffin-sized box?"

Elliot shook his head wildly. "I wasn't ever going to let her drown. She never saw my face. I was going to let it go on as long as possible, then let her go."

Tanner slammed his hand down on the desk. "You turned the water on high when we infiltrated the building."

"That was an accident, man!" Elliot squirmed in his seat. "I was trying to turn it *off* when I found out you guys were coming but you got there quicker than I expected. I panicked and ran. I never wanted that woman to die."

Whitaker walked forward and leaned all the way across the table into Elliot's space. "What about Shelby Durrant and Kelly Quinn? Did you *accidentally* kill them too?"

Elliot's eyes grew big. "Who? I don't know what you're talking about. I didn't kill anyone, man! I just wanted to mess with the cops. Get in and out of their system without them being able to trace me. That was how this all started. I wasn't going to let her drown."

Tanner glanced over at Whitaker. Damn it, he almost believed the kid.

"The other people, Elliot, your partners. Who are they?" Tanner demanded. "This is your one chance to do the right thing before your lawyer gets here and stops you from talking to everyone. Who are the other three people you're working with?"

"I promise I don't know. I don't know their names or what they look like or where they're doing their part of this. We met in an online chat room and—"

Whitaker's phone chimed multiple times in a row. "That's Pen. She must have—"

The door burst open and a uniformed police officer escorted a man in a suit inside.

"Are you talking to my client without his representation present?" The suited man raised an eyebrow so far it looked like it was about to find a new home in his hairline. "I'm going to have a field day with this."

Tanner crossed his leg and Whitaker leaned back casually against the wall. "No, no questioning. We aren't even Dallas PD, just fellow officers consulting from Colorado. So of course we wouldn't be questioning Mr. Webster, especially not once he'd asked to call you."

"Absolutely." Whitaker gestured to the camera. "I'm sure the recordings from this room will back us up. We were just in here keeping Elliot company. If he wants to make any sort of official statement, he'll need to make it with the Dallas PD, with you present, of course."

The lawyer glared at both of them, then turned to Elliot. "Is this true? They weren't harassing you into talking?"

Elliot studied his hands. "Everything's cool. But I should tell them—"

The lawyer held out a hand. "No. You say absolutely nothing."

"Tell us what, Elliot?" Tanner pushed. It would be worth the cost to save three lives.

"Do not talk to my client. If you have questions, you can refer them to me and I will advise him as to whether—"

"It's a chess game, man." Elliot ignored his lawyer and looked right at Tanner. "Chess."

"Mr. Webster!" the lawyer screeched. "I highly advise you not to say anything at all."

Elliot nodded. "Don't worry. I'm done."

Chapter Fourteen

They were barely outside the room when Penelope came rushing around the corner.

"We're okay," Whitaker reassured her. "Elliot actually covered for us a little bit when his lawyer arrived."

Penelope let out a sigh of relief. "When I saw the lawyer was Curtis Lowman I nearly had a heart attack. He's known for getting clients off the hook on technicalities. Did you guys get anything from Elliot?"

"Not anything of consequence," Whitaker said.

Tanner looked over at him. "I don't know about you, but I kind of believe the kid when he says he never planned to let Jean Adams drown."

They began walking back toward command central.

Penelope turned to them. "Did he have anything to say about the first two victims?"

Tanner ran a hand through his hair. "Look, he could be totally playing us, but I don't think he knew anything about them. I think for him this entire thing has been about seeing if he could get away with taunting the police. Some sort of game."

Whitaker nodded. "I think you're right—I don't think he ever planned to kill Jean Adams." Whitaker glanced at Penelope. "And unfortunately, I think he was telling the truth when he said he didn't know who or where his 'partners' are."

Penelope let out a curse. "Another dead end."

"We know Elliot met them online. Maybe Bree will find something." Tanner hoped it was true because they were running out of options pretty quickly.

"Leon is checking missing persons. Maybe that will get us something," Whitaker said.

Penelope reached for the door of the command area. "Let's see if we've gotten anywhere here. If not, I think we're going to need to question Jean Adams. I'd hoped to be able to wait—God knows she's been through enough. But we're running out of time."

The command center was still bustling with activity. Tanner's eyes automatically found Bree. He wasn't surprised to find her still working frantically at the computer like she had been when he'd left.

Leon met them as soon as they made it through the door.

"I found two other missing persons who fit the size and weight description. One—Betty Neighbors—actually lives in Waco. She's forty-five years old, divorced, lives alone. Her friends are not exactly sure how long she's been missing but definitely more than three days. I've already sent Morris and Gonzales there to interview."

Penelope nodded. "Good. Who's the other one?"

Leon grimaced. "Twenty-one-year-old Christina. We don't have a last name. She's been residing at a women's shelter out near Arlington and is working for tips at a local bar."

"Are you sure she's a legit missing person?" Whitaker asked. "Homeless? No real job? Maybe she just took off."

Leon nodded. "That was my thought at first, but evidently one of the ladies who works at the shelter has become close with Christina. Watches her eighteen-month-old daughter for Christina when she works."

They were all silent. Damn it, this case just kept getting worse.

"The lady at the women's shelter said there's no way Christina would've left the baby behind," Leon continued.

Penelope nodded. "Good. You and Whitaker

head over there and see if you can get any further details. And keep searching for other possible victims. Search outside state lines if you have to."

Leon nodded and walked over to the whiteboard, adding the pictures and details of Christina and Betty Neighbors.

Identifying possible victims was good for the case overall, but definitely didn't make it any easier to bear. Maybe in both cases it would end up being a mistake and the women would be found unharmed.

But Tanner had been in law enforcement long enough to know that wasn't likely.

"I think it's time to go visit Jean Adams," Penelope said.

Tanner nodded. "Anything she can remember might help. It's probably a good idea for you to talk to her. She might not be interested in being near any man right now."

She nodded. "Why don't you come with me? If there's any male she might want to talk to it would be you and Whitaker since you two saved her life."

Tanner didn't really want to go. He didn't want to leave Bree in case she needed him. But he also wanted to do everything in his power to get these other victims home safely.

"Let me just check with Bree and make sure she's okay."

Penelope raised an eyebrow, but just nodded. He jogged over to Bree's computer station.

"Any luck with Elliot?" she asked.

"No. I don't think he knows who or where the other victims or suspects are. He said he met them online. How's it going for you?"

She let out a frustrated sigh. "I thought I was going to have to do a lot of extrapolating and re-building. That Elliot would've destroyed data and not left it available online. But I was wrong. He left damn near everything there."

"You mean there's more information than you thought?"

"Exactly. Actually, it's kind of smart. There's so much for me to sort through that it would be easy to overlook something important."

"Do you want us to get you some help?"

She shook her head rapidly. "No. I have a system."

He knew much better than to try to make changes in any system she'd created.

"Plus," she continued, "I'm building some programs right now to help me filter through stuff. It's not foolproof, but it's propelling me through information quicker than sorting it all myself."

"Are you okay?"

"Yes, I have all the equipment I need."

Tanner trailed a finger down her cheek. "I mean, are *you* okay, freckles?"

Her shoulders slumped. "They think one of the victims is someone from a women's shelter," she whispered. "Someone with a baby."

"I know."

"That's like the women Cassandra and I help. As a matter fact, Christina reminds me of Marilyn, the lady Cass and I have been talking to about living at and running New Journeys once the renovations are done with our new building."

"*She's* going to live there, not you?"

She gave him a look that said she obviously found him deranged. "I live on the ranch. It never even crossed my mind for me to live at New Journeys. Unless you don't want me on the ranch any—"

He reached over and kissed her before she could finish the word. Kissed her hard, claiming her mouth in the most thorough of fashions. He didn't care that it was probably inappropriate or that they were in the middle of an important investigation.

"I want you there. Every single day, I want you with me," he said when he finally eased back from her lips.

"I'm not going anywhere."

"Good."

She glanced back at her computer. "Marilyn would never ever leave her kids. I don't think this Christina lady would either. I've got a really bad feeling that she might be one of our victims."

"We're going to get to her in time. To all of them in time. You just keep working. Penelope and I are going to go talk to Jean Adams. One way or another we're going to help these women."

"We do appreciate all your help you know," Penelope said as they pulled up at the hospital thirty minutes later. "You, Bree and Whitaker."

Tanner nodded. "Thanks, although I'm not doing anything anybody else on your team couldn't do. Bree is the one with the true talent here."

They got out of the car and walked toward the entrance. "She's something else."

Tanner couldn't stop his smile even if he had wanted to. "That, she definitely is."

"I know you guys are together, but after that kiss at the station… I'm assuming it's pretty serious."

Tanner gave a one-shoulderd shrug. "She's it for me. From the first moment I saw her, I knew she was my one."

Penelope gave a half smile. "Yeah, I get it. But Bree just doesn't seem like your type, you know? You guys are pretty opposite."

He and Bree were opposites. But that just

made them stronger. "She's not my type. She's my *everything*."

Penelope stopped walking for a second. "Wow. That's pretty firm."

"Yes." But *firm* wasn't even the right word. His feelings for Bree were completely unmovable.

She smiled and started walking again. "Can't blame a gal for double-checking."

They got Jean's room information and a doctor met them outside the door.

"How is she doing?" Penelope asked.

Dr. Yang looked at them with narrowed eyes. "Ms. Adams is doing well, physically. Emotionally, it's a different story. Are you sure this can't wait?"

"Believe me, we don't want to drag her through these details," Penelope explained. "And wouldn't if we had better options."

"We've got three other women's lives at stake," Tanner added. "And we're on a pretty tight deadline. No physical problems we need to know about? We understood hypothermia could be an issue."

"No, the water Jean was submerged in was actually temperature controlled. Lukewarm so as not to affect the body one way or another. She has pretty severe bruising on her wrists and ankles, and we're keeping her overnight to make sure nothing else pops up we need to be concerned with."

"And emotionally?" Penelope asked.

Dr. Yang tilted his head to the side. "About what you can expect from someone who's been through what she has. She's frightened. Angry. Her family is flying in from the East Coast but they haven't arrived yet. They weren't even aware she was missing."

"We'll be as brief and sensitive as we can. Tanner was the one who kept her above water until they could get her out of the box, so we're hoping she'll remember him a little fondly." Penelope reached for the door.

"And believe me," Tanner said, "we feel like we've gone through this with her. We're definitely sensitive to her suffering."

Dr. Yang walked in and introduced Penelope and Tanner.

Jean stared at Tanner. "I remember you. You were the one who helped keep my head out of the water."

Tanner smiled gently. "We're all very glad we made it in time."

Penelope took a step closer. "Jean, we normally would give you much longer to work through some of this before asking questions, but unfortunately you weren't the only victim. There are some other women, still trapped in situations exactly like yours. We're trying to do whatever we can to get to them."

Jean blanched, visibly shaking. "It's not that I don't want to help them, I'm just not sure I know how. I never even saw the guy who took me."

Penelope pulled up a picture of Elliot on her tablet. "This is the man who took you. Elliot Webster. Do you recognize him at all?"

Jean glanced at the picture, then looked away, staring over to the side. Tanner took a step closer. "He's currently in a holding cell, Jean," he explained gently. "There's absolutely no way he can hurt you. Just take a look at him and see if you recognize him from anywhere. That could help lead us in the right direction."

She finally glanced back at the tablet. "I—I'm not 100 percent sure, but he looks like a guy who has come by my coffee shop three or four times. Honestly, I never really paid much attention to him."

If he was just picking victims based on height and body size, seeing her at work a few times would've been all Elliot needed. He'd probably studied her a lot more than she was aware of, but there was no purpose in telling her that.

"Does that help?" she asked in a small voice.

Tanner smiled. "Absolutely."

Penelope brought up another couple of pictures on the tablet. Of Christina and Betty

Neighbors. "Do you happen to recognize either of these women?"

Jean studied these much more carefully. "No, I'm sorry."

"How about these two women?" Penelope showed her a picture of Shelby and Kelly when they were alive.

"No. Are they the other victims?"

Penelope shrugged. "They meet the potential criteria. That's all we know."

Jean's eyes found Tanner. "That's been driving me crazy. Trying to figure out why he took me. Why he put *me* in that box. Was it revenge? Was I mean to him? I try not to be rude to people, but maybe I was and I don't remember."

Jean's voice was becoming louder and more urgent. "Was it because of bad things I did? I cheated on my high school boyfriend. I lied in an interview for a job. Was it karma? Is that why he took me and put me in that box? What were the criteria?"

Tanner leaned down so he was face-to-face with Jean, stopping her tirade. "Do you want me to tell you what the criteria was? I'm afraid you might be a little bit disappointed, to be honest."

"Yes. Please tell me." Her voice was small.

"It's your size, Jean. Nothing more and nothing less than that. Nothing cosmic, no karma or revenge. It's the fact that you are five foot three and weigh 105 pounds."

"What?" Disbelief blanketed her features.

"He's telling the truth," Penelope said. "That's the common factor among all the victims. They all had to be roughly the same height and weight. Has nothing to do with anything else."

"You mean if I let myself put on the twenty pounds I wanted to over the last couple months he might not have chosen me? All I had to do was not work so hard at the gym?"

Tanner smiled at her. "Let it be a lesson to us all to have seconds of our meals as often as possible."

For the first time since they'd walked in, Jean actually smiled. "This helps. I'm still mad as hell and more than a little afraid of everyone I see, but at least knowing it wasn't something I did makes it all a little more bearable."

Tanner smiled back at her. "Good. Because it wasn't something you did that got you kidnapped, and definitely not anything you can be held accountable for."

"I feel like I haven't helped you at all. Do you have more questions for me?"

Penelope nodded. "Can you walk us through what happened the day you were kidnapped?"

Jean took a deep breath. "There's not a lot I can remember. I was closing the coffee shop with my manager. I decided to run by the bookstore before it closed. I was getting in my car when I felt a prick in my arm. I turned around to figure out what was going on, but everything got dizzy and none of my muscles seemed to work."

"Probably Midazolam or ketamine," Dr. Yang stated. "There weren't any traces left in her system, but that would be my bet."

"When I came to, I was in that box. It took me a while to realize the water was more than just annoying." Jean swallowed hard. "Eventually I realized the water was going to be what killed me. Then I couldn't stop thinking about it."

Jean talking about the water had been what had caused Bree to recognize the pattern, so that was a good thing.

They asked Jean some more questions, trying to see if she remembered anything that would help them, but the hours had all been a blur for her.

Tanner looked over at Penelope. Jean might have been able to help them if they were trying to catch Elliot. But if Elliot didn't know anything about the other suspects, it was doubtful Jean did either. They didn't want to upset her for no reason.

Finally, Penelope placed a business card on the table beside the hospital bed. "If you think of anything else, anything that you even get an inkling might be relevant, no matter how small, please call."

"Dr. Yang said your family is on their way," Tanner said. "Will you be okay until they get here?"

She nodded. "I just want to put all this behind me."

Tanner squeezed her hand as he and Penelope got ready to leave. "You will."

Chapter Fifteen

Bree had spent the last twelve hours filtering through all Elliot Webster's online data and was barely making a dent in it. The guy was a digital pack rat.

She'd passed the point of exhaustion hours ago. Now she was barely staying a half step above despair. Particularly because the victims, still being broadcasted at the top of every hour, were growing more and more desperate.

Bree was buried under data. It was so bad she'd even agreed to allowing help. Three of the people who worked under Jeremy were currently digging through Elliot's information also.

Bree had gone through all the critical data herself. For example, she'd found where Elliot had created a separate identity and credit card and used it to buy the ketamine he'd used to render Jean unconscious. Hell, she'd even found where he'd worked out the best way to encode and send the transmissions. How he'd arrived at the plan to use the fractal pattern.

It would all be great if they were trying just to convict Elliot. But it didn't do them much good in finding the other kidnappers or their victims.

Going through all this was like trying to find a needle in a haystack of needles. And now she needed to report in to Tanner and Penelope again and let them know she wasn't even a bit closer to finding anything useful.

Nobody cast any blame in her direction when she joined the team sitting around the conference room table fifteen minutes later and told them what was happening. But the frustration level was high.

"Elliot said he met these people online," Whitaker said.

Bree rubbed a hand across her face. "I'm sure he did considering he's been a part of roughly four thousand online conversations and has archived every single conversation in his data storage."

Penelope whistled through her teeth. "We need to get you more help to sort this information. Or maybe get you somewhere quieter to work. Or at least some damn headphones with music."

Bree shook her head. "No, I don't like music. I like the bustle of people around me, so I can ignore it. More help would be good, but I've already written programs to go through the chat rooms and look for a series of key words. That will be more efficient anyway."

"What sort of key words?" Tanner asked.

"Anything to do with the police, water, drowning. I put in the dimensions of the boxes they built and *polyethylene*, in case that would trigger something. I put in Jean Adams's name, Christina's name, Betty Neighbors's. I put in *fractal code* and *matrix grid pattern torus*."

She'd put in every single thing she could think of but so far there had been no results whatsoever.

She turned to Tanner. "I could've missed something. I had to have missed something." But for the life of her, she couldn't figure out what it was.

Those women were going to drown because she couldn't figure out how to find the necessary data in all Elliot's virtual junk.

I don't think you're working hard enough, Bethany. Obviously you're lacking an incentive to do your best work. Maybe this will help you.

"No, Mr. Jeter. I can do better. Please don't hurt Mom."

Michael Jeter just shook his head and tsked. "Your brain is stronger than this, Bethany. You just don't want it badly enough. You're allowing yourself to be unfocused and overwhelmed by superfluous details. I need you to focus."

He nodded his head to the man holding her

mother. Bethany tried not to vomit at the sickening sound of her mother's arm being broken, followed immediately by her screams.

"No!" Twelve-year-old Bethany tried to rush to her mother, but Jeter's heavy hand on her shoulder wouldn't let her move. He leaned down and whispered in her ear. "Now, are you ready to concentrate, or do you want to continue to make excuses? I need your best, Bethany. Is your best good enough?"

She nodded.

"It's time to think outside the box. If everything was simple, anyone could do it. The answer isn't where you expect it."

"I'm telling you, she's done. I'm taking her home."

Tanner was crouched beside her holding both of her hands in his, yelling at Penelope and Whitaker as Bree blinked her eyes open.

What the heck had just happened?

"Tanner?"

"Yeah, freckles, I'm here." He smiled at her before turning to glare back at the people sitting at the conference table. "You need some rest and to get away from all this."

She'd been having some sort of flashback. Everyone around the room was staring at her.

"No. I'm okay."

Tanner shook his head. "No, you're not okay.

This is not your job, and pushing yourself this way isn't healthy."

She shook her head, sitting up straighter in the chair. "I can have a breakdown later, then. Right now we need to do whatever we have to do to get these women out."

"Bree." Tanner's brown eyes were right in front of hers. "We all want to do our best, but there's one thing that we've all had to learn the hard way. Sometimes our best isn't good enough to save the victims."

"But…"

He trailed a finger down her cheek. "You're pushing yourself too hard if it's causing you to black out and have flashbacks."

"Tanner's right, Bree," Whitaker added. "About all of it. But especially about the fact that we can't always save the victims. None of us like to talk about it, but it's always a possibility."

She shook her head. "No. My best is good enough. It's time to think outside the box."

As much as she even hated the thought of it, Jeter had been right. He'd been right then and he was right now. Bree was being weak. Not properly motivated.

These women were going to *die* if she couldn't figure this out. Much worse than anything Jeter had ever done to her or her mother.

The answer isn't where you expect it.

But where? Where was it? There was something she was missing. "I haven't been looking in the right places."

"What do you mean?" Penelope asked.

"These guys met online, so we've been focusing our search in clubs, classes, chat rooms from the last two years. They would've had to communicate regularly."

Tanner stood beside her. "Yes, that's true."

"I've written half a dozen programs to look for key terms in any of those places. The people helping me have looked over it themselves. But we haven't found anything. He just left us with so much information. It feels like it's impossible to wade through it all."

"That probably means something is there," Tanner said.

She nodded. "You're right. And it's smart of him. It's the best sort of camouflage he could've picked. He's got hundreds of chat rooms about codes, engineering, patterns… And we haven't found anything there."

Penelope let out a sigh. "Maybe we need to talk to Elliot again. We won't get much because of the lawyer, but maybe I can bring the DA in on this super quick. See if we can strike a deal if Elliot is willing to talk right now."

Tanner shook his head. "That's not going to

be an easy process even if you have the DA on speed dial."

"It's like that little bastard said. It's a chess game," Whitaker said. "But we don't even have all the pieces."

Something clicked in Bree's mind. "Elliot said it was like a chess game? Specifically that?"

Tanner nodded. "Yeah. He mentioned chess when we were talking to him. Why?"

"Of course," she muttered. Elliot was smart. It made sense.

"What?" the other people in the room all asked at the same time.

"There's a chat room from his middle school chess club. I wanted to kill Elliot when I saw it. Why would anyone keep a chat room from a middle school chess club? We did a preliminary search of it, then immediately filed it as nonessential."

She turned to Tanner. "I have to go." It was time to think outside the box.

THE MIDDLE SCHOOL chess club chat room was the key.

It took Bree a few minutes to determine their code words and what they meant, but once she established that baseline, everything about the kidnapping plans was broken open.

"This is definitely it," she said.

Everyone was huddled around her workstation in a way that would have normally driven her crazy. It drove her a little crazy now, but she forced herself to ignore it. They all just wanted to finally hear some good news.

Bree was happy to be able to give it to them. When she knew what she was looking for, it wasn't difficult to find everything they had planned. They had discussed—using coded terms to make it seem like their discussion was about chess—the particulars about everything from the sizes of the boxes to the dimensions of the rooms where they would be held. The physics behind exactly how long it would take to fill the water coffins had been discussed at length.

"Damn," Whitaker muttered. "That's more details than Noah had building the ark."

Bree nodded. "Yes, their plans had to be exact. Otherwise we would've noticed right away that the boxes or the water levels were different. They know exactly when the victims will drown."

And it was six and a half hours from now.

"Get it on a timer," Penelope said. "That's our countdown clock. I'm going to trust their math."

Bree agreed. They hadn't left anything to chance.

There was some talk about victims, but not enough detail to give them positive IDs. That was disappointing for everyone.

But there was good news. The perps had all been checking in to the chat room regularly. They were starting to wonder where Elliot, or Number 3 as they called him, was, but no one was worried enough to panic yet.

"All we need is for one of them to hop in one more time," Bree said. "Once they do, I'll be able to decipher their location pretty quickly. I should also be able to clone their username and try to draw the others into coming online so that we can trace them too."

She felt Tanner's kiss at the top of her head. "We'll be ready."

"It's important that we move quickly, once I start to trace them. If we move too slowly, they may be able to warn one another."

"Got it," Penelope said. "We'll have to keep this on pretty tight radio silence. If the press gets hold of it they could tip off the killers."

Bree winced. "If that happens, the killers will go to ground. They would know better than to get back on the chat room."

And that would be it for the victims.

Everyone dispersed to get ready to go when Bree had a location.

"Why don't you take a break?" Tanner said. "Someone else can watch for entry into the chat room. I promise we will wake you up immediately if there's any activity."

"No, I can do this. I'm okay." She turned to look at him and could see the worry in his eyes. "Honestly. I know my little blackout incident was bad. Probably scary—"

"Not scary because I think you're weak. But scary because you shouldn't be pushing this hard. You were taught to work past your breaking point."

She reached up and grabbed his hand. "I haven't reached my breaking point yet. Having you here makes me stronger. I'm okay, I promise."

He studied her for a long moment, looking like he wanted to say more.

"I'm strong. I want to do this. I can do this."

He kissed her tenderly on the lips, just the softest of touches. "Good. Then let's catch these bastards and go home. We've got our own lives to get on with."

Chapter Sixteen

"Someone's in the chat room."

The command room fell completely silent at Bree's words. Tanner didn't move either. He knew the next few minutes were critical in getting the jump on the killers.

God, he couldn't be any prouder of Bree and how she'd handled herself and kept it together over the past few hours if… Hell, he just couldn't be any prouder.

The sooner he got the ring on this woman's finger and had them bound to each other for the rest of their lives, the better.

The grin that spread on her face a few minutes later just confirmed it all for Tanner.

"I've got him," she whispered. Once again, she rattled off an address.

"This isn't like last time," she said. "He's logging in live, but it has nothing to do with his transmissions of the victim. That means he might log back out at any moment. And there's no guarantee he's logging in at the same place he's keeping the victim."

Tanner turned to her. "You've been studying their interactions. Do you think you could fool him into getting him to tell you where he's holding her?"

"Maybe. But it might tip the others off. I could invite him into a private chat and see if I could get him to spill some details. I could act like I'm Elliot and I'm concerned about some mechanical or equipment issue."

Tanner looked over at Penelope. This was her call. If they spooked this guy and caused him to go to ground, they may not get another chance. And she already didn't trust Bree completely.

But Penelope nodded. "Do it. We're out of time."

Bree nodded. "I'll coax him into a private chat, clone this chat room so he can no longer see the real version and pretend to be him to the other two."

"That sounds a bit complicated," Whitaker said.

"It is. It's basically a shell game. We try to keep them distracted and our hands moving too fast for them to see what we're really doing. It's risky."

"Risky is better than nothing," Tanner said.

Bree didn't waste any more time. She immediately turned back to her computer and started doing what she needed to. Penelope sent Whitaker and Leon out to the address Bree had provided them. Maybe they would get lucky and be able to tail the guy the old-fashioned way.

Tanner moved to sit down by Bree in a show of silent support.

"He took the bait," she said a few minutes later, fingers still moving on the keyboard. "He's going into a private chat. I can't ask him questions outright, or he'll get suspicious. But I can at least clone the other chat so that he's locked out of that."

"Instead of asking him questions about his location, can you ask him if he's having problems with his water box? He doesn't have to tell you where he is. Just get him to go to the location and log in from there."

"You're brilliant, Tanner Dempsey. He has no idea I'm tracing him." She bit her lip. "Of course, if it was me, I'd already have multiple IDs with which I could log on. I'd never use the same one twice."

"That's why you're the smartest hacker on the planet, and this guy is just a bastard trying to get his jollies by tormenting as many people as possible. He wasn't expecting you. There's a difference between thinking you're the smartest person in the room and actually *being* the smartest person in the room."

She typed rapidly. "I'm telling him that I'm Elliot and that I've been offline because I'm having a problem with the water box. That I've been manually filling it according to their calculations, but that I think there's a flaw in the building plans."

They waited a few seconds to see if their prey would fall for it.

He did.

"Okay, he's logging out of the main chat room and logging into the private one. I'm cloning the private one so if he goes back in, unless he specifically looks to see if it's a clone, he won't realize anything has changed."

"So Leon and Whitaker are free to pursue?"

"Yes, but they need to be careful not to spook him."

"They'll stay back, just keep him in sight. In case this plan doesn't work, we need a backup."

She nodded and began typing again. "Okay, I'm asking him if he's noticed a problem with the box. Telling him that I almost missed it and that he needs to double-check as soon as possible."

She stopped typing and stared at the screen.

"Do you think he bought it?"

"Honestly, I'm not sure. I dropped my message and left. I figured it looked less suspicious if I wanted to talk even less than him. If the roles were reversed it would reassure me a little."

He squeezed her hand. "Smart."

"Okay, he's dropped out of the private chat. This is good. We need to be ready to go. Hopefully he's going to get back on in a few minutes to say that his box did not have the same problem as mine. And when he does that, we'll have a location of the victim."

Now it was a waiting game.

Penelope walked over to them a few minutes later. "Bad news. The address was empty by the time Leon and Whitaker got there."

"Then this is our only shot," Bree said.

Tanner nodded. "It's going to work."

She didn't have to say anything for him to know she wasn't so sure about that. But just because it wouldn't trick her didn't mean it wouldn't fool damn near everybody else on the planet.

"It's going to work," he said again. "Let's be ready to go."

Bree nodded. "I'll come with you, if he gets back in the chat room. Just in case we need to reel him in further. Or if not, I'll be working remotely on the other two."

The silence fell heavy over the room for nearly twenty minutes.

Bree finally slammed her hand on the desk. "Yes!" she shouted. "He just logged in and said he checked the water box. That should mean he's at the location."

She rattled off an address.

This time Penelope didn't look confused. "That's on the outskirts of town. A lot of abandoned buildings. If I was going to try to keep a kidnapping quiet, that's where I would do it. Let's go. We'll have Leon and Whitaker meet us there."

Bree grabbed her laptop and was right behind Tanner as he followed Penelope to the car. As soon as Bree got into the back seat she began typing away again.

"I'm working on the other two," she said. "If they are open for the same sort of trick we used with this guy then this could be easier than I thought."

Penelope was on the phone with Whitaker, working out details. The building was an abandoned motel and SWAT was meeting them there. It was too big for the four of them to canvass on their own.

They were reaching the edge of town, only a couple of miles from their location, when Bree spoke again.

"According to GPS, there's a coffee shop at the corner of the next block. You should leave me there. You don't want to have to worry about me as you're doing your bad-guy stuff, and the coffee shop will have Wi-Fi, which will allow me to work faster."

Penelope glanced over at Tanner and he gave a nod. He wanted Bree kept clear of all this.

"Fine, but we have to keep moving." Penelope responded.

Tanner turned and shot Bree a concerned look in the back seat. He'd rather get her settled himself.

Bree just rolled her eyes. "I'm more than capable of walking myself into a coffeehouse without getting into any trouble. Go do what you need to do."

Sure enough, when Penelope stopped the car a block later Bree was out the door with a quick "Good luck."

The door had barely shut behind her before Penelope was taking off again.

"We're dealing with a much bigger area than we were with Elliot, and we don't have any details," she said. "We'll have SWAT, but the guy may kill the victim outright if he gets spooked."

"How do you want this to play?"

"Room by room search," she said. "Methodically and orderly."

A few seconds later his phone beeped. He looked down at the message and smiled.

"Bree just sent us the building plans for that address."

"I have to admit she is pretty damn useful."

Tanner laughed as he studied the plans. "That and a lot more."

They parked at the spot where Penelope had told Leon and Whitaker to meet. They were already there. Tanner got out of the car while Penelope answered a call.

"We just got building plans from Bree," Whitaker said.

"Knowing her, the entire SWAT team got it too," Tanner said.

Penelope finished her call and turned back to them. "Chief doesn't want anybody who is not official Dallas PD going into the building, in case things get ugly. Sorry guys."

Tanner didn't like it, but he could understand it.

"We can still be used strategically. There are a lot of exits to this place." Tanner pointed to the building schematics on his phone. "I can camp out in the alleyway in case the perp slips past you and runs like Elliot did."

Whitaker nodded. "And I can cover the fire exit in the back in case he makes a run for it that way."

Penelope nodded. She handed them walkie-talkies. "Yeah. If this guy gets away, the first thing he'll probably do is warn the others."

"Roger that. Priority is to stop him before he makes contact. And hopefully by the time we're done here, Bree will already have the location of the other two victims," Tanner said.

The SWAT team showed up, parking a block away, and they all took their positions. Tanner made his way to the alley he'd be covering. He'd much rather be part of the action inside the building, but knew this case was going to be delicate enough without having unauthorized personnel as part of the takedown. Better to do as much as possible by the books. Unless it came down to truly dire situations, he would stay out of it.

He was in the alley, finding the best vantage point for the exit that led his way, when his phone buzzed in its holder. He glanced down to see the caller, thinking it might be Bree, but it was Gregory Lightfoot.

Tanner press the receive button. "Greg. Kind of a bad time. Can I call you back?"

"Tanner, this is an emergency. I just found out the prison bus transferring Michael Jeter crashed pretty badly a couple of hours ago. It was chaos. Some prisoners killed, others hurt bad."

"And Jeter?"

"Right now no one is exactly sure where he is."

Chapter Seventeen

Tanner let out a vile curse. "What exactly are you saying? That Jeter escaped?"

Because two hours was definitely more than enough time for Jeter to have gotten to where Bree was right now *alone*.

"I've already made some calls." Greg's voice was rapid and hoarse. "I've explained the situation and the prison warden on-site at the crash assures me that no prisoners are missing. The issue was, with the multiple injuries, some of them severe, they had to send prisoners to multiple hospitals. But all of them went in handcuffs and all the hospitals are aware of their criminal status."

That made Tanner feel marginally better, but not enough to be willing to leave Bree alone. Not until he knew for sure that Jeter wasn't out in the open.

"Why weren't we notified right away?"

"I was in court, and my assistant couldn't get ahold of me. The moment she did, I called you.

I'm staying on top of it as much as possible and will report back to you as soon as I have any more details."

"Do." It wasn't a request. When it came to Bree's safety Tanner was not going to worry about being polite. "Immediately, Greg. No matter how big or small."

"I will."

Tanner disconnected the call without another word.

He immediately called Bree and tried not to panic when the call went to voice mail. She never answered her phone if she had an option.

He texted her instead.

Problem with Jeter. Stay inside the coffeehouse until I or an officer comes for you. Call me.

He waited a few seconds for a response, fighting back a little more panic when there was none. She was focused. Might be in a situation talking to the other kidnappers online where every second counted and couldn't answer him.

Tanner tried to focus on the facts. The prison warden had assured Greg no prisoners had escaped. There was no reason to think that wasn't true. And even if Jeter *had* managed to escape unnoticed, how would he even know where Bree was? Until thirty minutes ago *they* didn't even know where Bree would be, so there was no way Jeter could've set a trap for her.

Somehow none of this reassured him.

He placed a call to Whitaker. He couldn't leave here, since he didn't have a car anyway, but he needed to get eyes on Bree immediately.

Whitaker picked up on the first ring. "What's wrong?"

Whitaker knew Tanner well enough to know that he would not be calling in the middle of an important operation if it wasn't important.

"I just got word that Michael Jeter is currently MIA. There was a prison transfer bus accident with multiple injuries and right now we're not exactly sure where he is, although there is no report of any escapees."

"What do you need?"

"I can't get to Bree myself, but I'd feel much better knowing we have eyes on her. I know there's no reason to think Jeter is anywhere nearby, but…"

"I'll get a couple of uniformed officers over to the coffeehouse right away. Better safe than sorry."

"Thanks, man. I didn't want to leave my post, but Bree didn't answer my text and everything about Jeter makes me uncomfortable."

"No need to explain," Whitaker said. "Not to

mention, we need Bree more now than ever. I'll have somebody on her in less than five minutes."

Tanner disconnected and immediately tried Bree's cell again, biting back a curse when the call went straight to voice mail again and his text still went unread.

He was about to try again when the walkie-talkie in his hand clicked on.

"The perp is on the run," Penelope announced. "Repeat, perp is on the run. He sneaked out some back door and is probably headed in your direction, Tanner."

"Roger that. I'm ready."

"No weapons unless you perceive a direct threat to you."

"Got it." Definitely didn't make things easier, but it wasn't Tanner's policy to shoot a fleeing suspect in the back unless he was a direct threat to those around him.

Less than thirty seconds later Tanner heard the door open in front of him. He immediately brought up his weapon. He wasn't going to shoot the guy, but the guy didn't need to know that.

And, damn, this one was definitely much bigger than Elliot Webster. Guy looked like a linebacker.

"Police," Tanner shouted. The perp didn't need to know that Tanner wasn't *Dallas* police. "Stay where you are and put your hands where I can see them."

The guy didn't even slow down. He was running at Tanner at full speed.

Damn it, Tanner did not have time for this. He didn't want to chase this guy down the block and waste valuable time that could be used making sure Bree was safe. He didn't care if the guy looked like he was going to run over Tanner. Tanner had played some football in his time too.

He knew how to take a hit. And he definitely knew how to keep an opponent from reaching his objective. In high school that had been keeping a running back from scoring a touchdown.

Now it was keeping this guy from escaping the alley.

Tanner bent his knees and braced himself for the impact as the guy paid no heed to the warning of the gun and continued to barrel toward him. At the last moment Tanner dropped even lower in his stance and flew toward the guy, tackling him low in the legs.

The guy wasn't expecting the move from Tanner, obviously betting on the fact that Tanner wouldn't shoot and never considering Tanner wouldn't just get out of the way.

The bigger they are the harder they fall was a saying for a reason, and this guy hitting the ground hard just further proved it.

Penelope had asked him not to shoot the perp, and Tanner didn't. But that didn't stop him from clocking the guy in the jaw with his elbow when he tried to stand back up and get away again.

"You have the right to remain silent. You're under arrest, you son of a bitch."

The guy grunted and threw a punch at Tanner. He saw stars as the guy's meaty fist caught him on the jaw.

Tanner returned the favor with a blow of his own, flipping the guy over while he was dazed. "You have the right to remain silent, although I personally hope you'll sing like a canary."

Tanner didn't even care that he was making a mockery of the Miranda rights. Somebody was going to have to reread them to him when they arrested him for real. Tanner was basically babysitting until then. Babysitting a six-foot-two, two-hundred-pound baby struggling to get away from him, but babysitting nonetheless.

It was only a few more seconds before some members of the SWAT team burst through the door and ran up to Tanner, taking over the arrest process. Tanner was more than happy to let them do it.

Whitaker came rushing around the corner, weapon drawn. He holstered it when he saw the SWAT team had the situation well under control.

Whitaker brought his walkie-talkie closer

to his mouth. "Penelope, we've got the suspect in custody."

"Good," the woman responded. "We've got the victim. She's alive and still out of danger with the water. We've got it turned off, but evidently this guy didn't know we were coming like Elliot did."

Tanner brought up his own walkie-talkie. "Penelope, I've got to go. I have reason to think Bree might be in danger." He looked over at Whitaker.

The man shook his head. "The officers should've already been in contact with her and reported back. I haven't heard anything."

The walkie-talkie clicked back on. "You two go. There's nothing you can do now anyway. I think we caught this guy before he could contact the others, so we definitely need to find Bree to figure out our next move."

Tanner and Whitaker were running for the car before she even finished the sentence. As soon as they got inside, they were both on the phone—Tanner trying Bree's cell again and Whitaker calling the officers who should have found her already.

Tanner once again got no response and whatever Whitaker heard had him cursing.

"Well, did you talk to any of the employees and ask if they'd seen her?"

Whitaker didn't like whatever the officer answered and Tanner could feel his heart begin to hammer.

"We'll be there in less than five minutes. Make sure you've checked every possible spot in that café that she could be. Bathrooms. Storage room. Bree can sometimes want to have privacy, so check the places that might seem unusual to you."

What Whitaker was saying was right, but why would Bree be hiding when it had been such a short time? Why would she leave the safety of the coffeehouse at all?

She wouldn't. She'd be working.

It was all Tanner could do not to yell at Whitaker to drive faster. The man was driving as fast as he could. Instead, Tanner redialed Greg's number.

Greg didn't waste time when he answered. "Tanner. I'm still working on it. The last thing I heard was that Jeter was sent to Parkland Hospital. I've sent one of my people over there to confirm. But the word is still that none of the prisoners escaped. Is Bree okay?"

"We can't get ahold of her and she's not where she's supposed to be."

Greg let out a curse. "As soon as my guy arrives at the hospital I'll give you a call back."

"Thanks." Tanner disconnected the call as they pulled up in front of the coffeehouse and he rushed inside. The uniformed officers were talking to the staff behind the counter. Tanner and

Whitaker double-checked all the possible rooms where Bree could be.

She wasn't there.

Fear emptied into him like an icy downpour.

He pulled a picture from his phone and held it up in front of the manager. "Her. Was she in here? Did she leave with anyone?"

"Yeah, I remember her," the manager said. "She was mad because the internet hasn't been working right today."

The tightness in Tanner's chest eased just slightly. Not having working internet would be one of the few reasons why Bree would have left of her own volition. He pulled out his phone and dialed hers again.

It was only because the rest of the room was so quiet that they heard the vibrating of a phone in the back corner as Tanner called. Whitaker ran back there.

"It's her phone."

The manager nodded. "Yeah, that's where she was sitting." Tanner disconnected the call and walked over to the corner. He and Whitaker both looked around.

"There's no sign of a struggle," Whitaker said. "And somebody would've seen if Jeter was here and tried to take her out."

Tanner nodded. "And no internet here means

she could've left on her own. It's the one reason she would."

They both looked up as the bell chimed on the door as someone entered.

The ball of ice around his heart eased when he saw it was Bree, laptop held in one arm, typing with the other hand, screen up to her face, completely unaware that everyone in the coffeehouse was looking at her. She literally nearly ran into Whitaker before she even looked up.

"Excuse me, I left my phone and I—" She finally realized it was them. "Oh, hey. What are you guys doing here?"

Tanner scrubbed a hand over his face. This was Bree. He'd seen her get lost more than once while working on computers. Couldn't remember to do even the most basic of tasks like feed herself or go to sleep. He couldn't get frustrated with her for being herself.

The most important thing was that she was safe and he was going to make sure she stayed that way.

"We caught the bad guy and got to the victim. The victim is going to be okay and we don't think the perp was able to get word to anyone else," Tanner said, taking the computer from her, setting it on the table and pulling her against his chest.

She was fine. Thank God, she was okay.

Bree didn't question his actions, just snuggled against him, wrapping her arms around his waist. "Good. I've sent separate messages to the other two. As long as they are not conferring with each other separately, I think they both will eventually take the bait."

She finally reached back and took a good look at him. "Are you sure you're okay? I thought you said the woman was alive." She reached up and smoothed her small thumb across his brow. "Why so worried?"

He couldn't hide this from her. They'd come too far in their relationship, in their trust in one another, to keep something as critical as Jeter's whereabouts from her. Tanner respected her too much for that.

But damn he didn't want to tell her that her worst nightmare was unaccounted for.

"It's Jeter. There was a crash of the prison bus and no one is completely sure where Jeter is."

Chapter Eighteen

Bree felt like the entire world was falling out from under her. Tanner was saying other stuff, stuff meant to reassure her that Jeter wouldn't get to her.

If Michael Jeter was out, there was nowhere on earth that he couldn't get to her.

She'd spent much of her life running from him and the Organization, and that was before he'd known for sure she was alive. Now that he knew for certain she was and she'd helped get him arrested, he would never stop hunting her.

Her first inclination was to run. She was far from the emergency bug-out bag she had stashed at the ranch house, but she knew enough to know how to make herself disappear in a crowd. She could get completely off the grid and maybe find a way to evade Jeter long term.

She was actually turning toward the door, instinct to flee riding her harder than anything else, when Tanner's hands came up and cupped her face.

"Breathe, freckles."

Bree sucked in air and realized she had, in fact, been holding her breath.

"You're not going to run," he continued. "You're not alone anymore."

Her hands wrapped around his wrists like they were her lifeline. "Tanner, I know I've talked about Jeter, but you really don't know the truth of it. I'm putting everyone in danger if he's out. You. Your family. Everyone in Risk Peak. He'll hurt them all."

He brought his face closer to hers so it was the only thing she could see. "You're not alone in this. Never again. No running, especially not until we have all the facts about Jeter."

He stayed there, blocking out everything else, surrounding her with his presence until the panic finally melted just enough that she could process what he was saying.

He was right. They didn't have all the information. They didn't even know for sure where Jeter was.

And she couldn't run now. If she ran, there were two women who would die. Bree was the only one who could find them.

She sucked in a shaky breath. "I know—you're right. I panicked. I won't run."

His forehead dropped against hers. "Nobody blames you for a little bit of panic. But whatever we decide to do, we do it together, okay? No running."

She nodded. "And I've still got to do whatever I can to help these women. I can't leave them to die."

"And I'm going to be with you every single minute. When I say you're not alone, I'm not just talking about the long-term, big stuff. I'm talking about *everything*."

And this was why she loved this man. Because she knew everything he said to her was the truth. She nodded again and he kissed her gently.

"Let's get you back to the police station. That will definitely be the safest place for you."

She grabbed her computer as he led her out to the car, Whitaker handing her the cell phone she'd left behind on the way. She winced at the multiple missed calls and texts from Tanner.

Whitaker and Tanner kept her between them, both looking out for possible threats as they stepped outside and walked quickly to the car. Tanner's firm hand on her arm—the other one resting close to his weapon—told her exactly how much this Jeter thing was weighing on him.

The uniformed officers gave them an escort back to the police station. Once again, Bree was quickly ushered inside.

Tanner didn't let down his guard even once they were inside the building. He was taking the threat of Jeter seriously. If Jeter was out and had access to a computer, he could hack into the Dallas PD system and make it look like he was employed there. He could have a badge and access pass within minutes.

The thought had her panic inching back up. Jeter could be anywhere.

Tanner was probably afraid the man would try to kill her. Bree wasn't. Jeter wanted her for himself. *Alive.*

Once they made it back to the command room Tanner relaxed a little bit. At least here all the faces were familiar. A stranger would be much more noticeable.

The clock at the front of the wall caught Bree's attention. It was counting down the minutes until the last two women would be covered in water and drown. Less than three hours.

Bree was going to have to trust Tanner to keep her safe from Jeter. She was going to need every spare minute to figure out where these last two women were.

"I've got to work. We're out of time," she whispered to him.

He gave her a brief nod before his eyes moved back up, gauging the room. "You work. I promise I will keep you safe."

Tanner had always done that. Even from that first moment when he'd caught her shoplifting formula and diapers, and had no idea who she was or what she needed, he'd always protected her. He protected her when it meant putting his own life in danger and he'd protected her even when it meant he might lose everything. There was not one bit of her that had any doubt he would protect her now.

She sat down and placed the laptop next to the desktop computer she'd been working on here. Her life was in Tanner's hands.

The lives of two other women were in hers.

IF TANNER HAD thought the circumstances under which Bree was working before were bad, it was nothing compared to watching her trying to work with the threat of Jeter hanging over her.

The killers couldn't have done anything more to split her focus if they had gone and broken Jeter out of prison themselves. It was one of the very few things that would slow Bree down.

But it still wasn't slowing her down much.

She was writing code faster than most people could write their name. And she was doing it on the fly, coming up with ways to try to trap the kidnapers, backing them into a virtual corner.

She'd explained just a little bit as the first program she wrote was uploading, then had warned him he probably didn't want to know exactly what the program was going to do.

She was right. He didn't care if the program was illegal, not with that clock counting down the minutes those women had left.

The first thing Bree had had to do was reconfigure the live footage that was to come from the victim they'd just rescued. If it didn't go live, the other two kidnappers would know the police were onto them.

The suspect they'd arrested—the linebacker—was proving quite a bit more interesting than Elliot Webster.

The man's name was Rory Gresham. He was thirty-four years old and pretty much a laundry list of trouble. When he was twenty-one he had applied to work for Dallas PD, but had been rejected when he couldn't pass the psychological profile test. He'd gone on to attend Texas A&M, like Elliot, also studying engineering, and had held a good job at the City Planner's office until about a year ago when he'd been fired for aggressive behavior against his colleagues.

After the tackle they'd shared in that alley, Tanner felt quite familiar with Rory's aggressive tendencies.

Rory had spent the last year with time on his hands and revenge on his mind.

Based on the information in the chat room Bree

had found, it looked like Rory was the mastermind behind most of this plan. He definitely wanted to stick it to the Dallas PD and to the Dallas city government in general.

He was in custody now, Penelope questioning him with his lawyer present. His victim, Alice Cornick, had been taken to the hospital but, like Jean Adams, didn't seem to have any serious physical injuries.

If Tanner had to bet, he would say that Rory was probably the one responsible for the deaths of Shelby and Kelly Quinn. The man wanted to make sure everything was perfect, that there was nothing in the late stages of the game that he would have to factor into consideration. By all accounts, in both his college classes and at his job, he'd been considered brilliant, if not able to work with others.

According to Penelope, all he'd said so far was that the Dallas PD could go to hell. They should have hired him when they had the chance.

Bree's shoulders were getting more and more tense as she worked. He'd hoped that the victim they got to next would be Christina, the woman from the shelter who reminded Bree so much of her friend. That would take at least a little of the pressure off her.

When his phone rang in his pocket and he saw

it was Greg Lightfoot, he stepped away from Bree's desk so he wouldn't disturb her.

"Talk to me, Greg."

"Tanner, I'm at Parkland Hospital myself. I can confirm that Michael Jeter is in custody."

Tanner felt the pressure that had been sitting on his chest like a rock ease at Greg's words.

"You have eyes on him yourself?"

"That's an affirmative. Jeter's face was burned pretty bad. But I personally sat there and watched the US Marshals run Jeter's fingerprints. And then I had them do a match to a physical print, not a computer match. I'm well aware of what Jeter can do to all things computer."

"Damn fine thinking, Greg."

"It's him, Tanner. And given the state he's in, Bree does not have to worry about him coming after her anytime soon."

"The hospital is notorious for less security. Make sure whoever is standing guard is aware that any remaining friends Jeter has might use this opportunity to try to break him out."

"Will do. Are you and Bree working this drowning case?"

Tanner swallowed a curse. "Did news break about it?"

"Yeah. Not a lot of details, but that's some messed-up stuff."

"Believe me, you don't know the half of it.

Thanks for going to the hospital and checking yourself, Greg. Let me know if you learn anything else."

Tanner discussed a few more details with Greg, then disconnected the call. He immediately walked over to Bree.

"I just got off the phone with Greg. Do you want the good news or the bad news first?"

Her head tilted to the side. "Good news."

"Greg went to the hospital himself and confirmed that Jeter was indeed there. He's got some burns on his face, but Greg watched as they ran his fingerprints and compared them to a physical copy. No computers."

For the first time, Bree actually stopped her typing and gave him her full attention. "It was really him? The prison bus accident was really just an accident with really crappy timing for us?"

He nodded. "I know it's hard to believe, but in this case, yes. I think it might have all just been a coincidence. Of course, I'm making damn well sure everyone knows what a danger Jeter and his remaining friends are. But right now it looks like he's in pretty bad condition anyway. Couldn't be much of a risk to you even if he wanted to."

She nodded and let out a deep breath. "Okay. Then Jeter is officially a problem for another day."

"Yup." He cupped her cheek. "But whatever

day Jeter decides to show up I'm going to be right next to you waiting for him."

Her smile made him want to pull her into his arms, but they had the bad news to deal with first.

"But that was the good news. Bad news is, word is out about the drowning cases."

Bree turned back to her computer. "Actually, that was me that leaked it. Now that we have a little information about Rory Gresham, I'm using the press to play off the last two kidnappers. I'm talking to both of them separately, pretending with each to be the other one."

"Are you sure they're not going to kill the victims outright and just make a run for it?"

She let out a little sigh. "That's my biggest concern. Right now, I'm in discussion with both of them on the pros and cons of keeping the women alive."

He whistled through his teeth. Not that he didn't trust her, but that was a lot of pressure and if it went wrong, could mean a lot of guilt for Bree. He didn't want that for her. "What can I do to help?"

"I'm hoping the news report of Gresham's arrest will spark some sort of panicked action. It's the only play I have left. We're down to the last forty-five minutes."

Damn it. That was so little time. "Freckles, listen."

She held up a hand. "No, don't give me the

consolation talk now. Not while we can still save them. I'm going to damn well try everything in my power to get them out."

She was right. He should not be treating this as if they'd already lost these women. "I'm sorry. It's not that I don't have faith in you…"

"I get it, hot lips. You're you and want to protect me. And I love you for it. But right now…" Her eyes grew big. "I'll be damned."

"What?" She had diverted her attention from her main computer back over to the laptop.

"It worked. One of them just panicked and made a pretty rookie mistake. I set up a side channel attack on the very slim chance that someone would panic and one of them did and just triggered it."

"English, freckles."

She typed for a few seconds. "I know where victim number three is."

Chapter Nineteen

Everybody flew into action the moment Bree had an address. Whitaker immediately got Penelope from where she was still interrogating Rory Gresham.

Nobody recognized the address because it was so far out of town. By the time Penelope came rushing into the room Leon had it pulled up on a map.

"What do we got?" Penelope asked.

"Looks like a damn farmhouse," Leon answered. "Definitely not industrial like the warehouse or the empty hotel."

"Perp doesn't need that big of a space," Tanner said. "Just somewhere where he could get the vic in without people noticing. A barn would definitely work."

Whitaker looked over at Penelope. "It's going to take every bit of thirty minutes just to get out there. And we've still got the fourth victim."

"I've got our fourth kidnapper talking to me,"

Bree said. "He's a little more guarded. Prickly. He didn't like finding out who Rory Gresham was. I think the fourth guy feels like he's been used for someone else's agenda."

Whitaker rolled his eyes. "That's what happens when you jump into bed with people you don't even know. Might want to find out a little bit more about them before committing to their sick little experiments."

Tanner couldn't help but agree.

Bree shrugged. "I'll be the first to admit that I'm not great at reading people, but it's like this fourth kidnapper feels personally betrayed by Gresham. Scorned almost. Wait, I…" She faded off. "Let me try something."

Bree sat down and began typing on her laptop. Penelope looked over her head at him.

"We've got to leave right now or we won't make it to that farm in time to save the third victim. Whitaker and I will head to the farm, you and Leon keep working number four and move as soon as you've got actionable intel."

Tanner nodded. "I'm not leaving Bree alone."

Penelope let out a frustrated sigh. "Do you think she's not safe here in the middle of the police department?"

"Nothing against any sort of security here, but Bree stays with me."

He wasn't still on full alert, but until he had a

chance to check on Jeter himself and make sure the people guarding him knew what they were dealing with, Tanner wasn't letting Bree out of his sight. Not that he didn't trust Greg, but he'd seen Jeter's Organization at work and he wasn't willing to risk Bree's life on anything, particularly at this.

"Fine." Penelope turned to Leon. "Make sure you bring extra backup then."

She and Whitaker were rushing out the door without another word.

There were twenty-eight minutes left until the victims drowned.

Bree was frantically pounding away at her keyboard.

"There it is." Bree pointed to a chat room window that popped up on her screen.

"What is that?" Leon asked. "It looks like something from a dating site."

"That's exactly what it is," Bree responded. "And it predates their group getting together. And it's with Rory Gresham and kidnapper four."

"I totally don't understand what we're talking about here," Leon said, studying the screen. "Two of them were dating? So Gresham is gay?"

Bree shook her head. "No. I think suspect number four is a woman. On the dating site, Gresham talked about wanting to prove himself. That once he pulls off this little operation, he would get taken seriously and would be able to move forward with the relationship. But now the fourth suspect realizes Gresham never really had any plan for them to be in a relationship. Rory was just using her—using all of the kidnappers—to get his revenge on the city of Dallas."

Both Tanner and Leon shook their head.

"What I don't know is how to use this information to get her to tell me where she is," Bree continued.

"Are you relatively sure she only knows Rory Gresham and not the other kidnappers?"

Bree shrugged. "Honestly, she probably didn't even know Rory. Just what he told her online. There's no indication that she knows the other two outside of their main chat room. I've tried everything I can think of to get her to tell me where she is. Now that the information about Rory has come out, she has receded even further."

Bree rubbed a hand across her face. "I don't think I'm going to be able to get to her, or the victim, in time. She doesn't want to talk about anything to do with the plan or the box or anything."

"That's because right now none of that stuff is what's important to her," Tanner said. "She's got her mind on other things. Things of the heart."

Bree's green eyes pinned him. "She does?"

He pointed to the chat room box. "She's thinking about the fact that the man she spent a lot of time talking to and investing in, lied to her. Try talking to her as a woman. Remember how you felt when you thought maybe Penelope was attracted to me?"

He was right. Bree needed to talk to her woman to woman. Her hand began flying over the keyboard again. "If I pretend to be kidnapper three and tell her that Rory made those same promises to me? Maybe that will get her to drop her guard. I'm going to have to say it in the public room, but she's the only one left checking that."

Bree's hands flew across the keyboard. "For the record, if you have been promising yourself to both me and Penelope, I definitely would be willing to stop what I was doing and make sure you felt my wrath."

Tanner chuckled. "Let's hope it's true with this person too."

"I'm telling her that I can't believe what I just heard about Rory. That he had made me feel special and that it was all a sham. That I had agreed to this plan for personal reasons with him, not for his agenda."

Tanner nodded. "Good. That's good."

A few seconds later Bree smiled. "She's on."

They all watched the screen as the suspect typed.

I feel like Rory lied about everything.

Bree was quick to respond.

I thought he wanted to be in a relationship with me. I feel like he was just using me.

You female irl?

"She's asking me if I'm female in real life," Bree explained.

"This is it. You need to get her to move into a communication with you that we can track," Tanner said.

Bree muttered a curse. "I need two minutes to write a shell program that will bounce off a private chat room and lead us to her. Talk to her while I write it."

Bree sprinted over to her desktop computer and Tanner sat down in her place, praying he wouldn't say something to scare the suspect off.

Yes. Female irl. Rory and I met on an online dating site. I thought he was into me.

Same. Bastard has been using all of us.

"Hurry, freckles," Tanner muttered. "I'm running out of things to say to her."

"Forty-five seconds."
Tanner strained to find something to say.

Did you meet Rory irl?

It felt strange to use the initials, but it would be a dead giveaway if he wrote out the words.

No. We agreed to meet after. U?

Bree came sprinting back over. "I've got it. Let me talk to her."
Bree's fingers flew over the keys.

Mind if we switch over to pm? I don't trust this chat anymore.

Bree put the link out for the private chat.
"Now we see if it works." Tanner looked up at the clock. They had less than twenty minutes left. It was going to be close, and that was if the suspect was actually with the victim.
Two minutes that seemed like an eternity ticked by.
"I don't think she's falling for it. I made it look real but if she pokes at it too hard, she's going to see what it really is."
Another minute went by. And Tanner began to worry Bree was right. She had the open chat

room right in front of her. "All I need is for her to get on one time and we'll have her."

Finally some words popped onto the screen.

I'm here.

Bree's hand flew over the keys once again. And a dozen seconds later she had an address.

"That's fifteen minutes away," Leon said.

Once again they were dashing for the door.

Leon drove, siren blazing, cutting off traffic everywhere he could in order to make up time.

Both Tanner's and Leon's phones buzzed at the same time. Leon didn't even gaze at his, eyes focused on the road.

It was a message from Whitaker. Tanner couldn't help but smile as he read it.

"Whitaker and Penelope made it to the third victim in time. It was Christina. She's safe."

Bree let out a little sigh of relief. "I know no one's life is worth more than another, but I'm glad a baby girl is not going to grow up without her mother because of this."

Tanner squeezed her hand. "How about we spoil everything for Rory Gresham and rescue this last woman too?"

"Has anything changed about the location?" Leon asked.

Bree typed for just a couple of seconds then a frown marred her features.

"What?" Tanner asked.

"The channel is still open, but she's not talking. She hasn't said anything since letting me know she was there. It's just odd that she would get in there and then not say anything else. Even when I asked her a question."

Tanner looked over at Leon. "This could be a trap."

He gave a brief nod without taking his eyes off the road. "It doesn't matter. We are out of time for stealth."

In less than two minutes they were screeching to a halt in front of a small house. It backed up to the woods, which was probably what had allowed the kidnapper to get the victim inside without being seen. It wouldn't have been easy, but not impossible.

Bree was climbing out the door as soon as the car stopped.

"Where are you going?" Tanner asked.

She looked at him like he was crazy. "There's no way you're sending Leon in there by himself, especially after what you guys just said about this possibly being a trap. And I know you're not letting me stay by myself in the car, so I'm coming with you."

Tanner bit off a curse. "Do you really think it's safer for you inside there?"

"I refuse to be a liability to you. I know you have an extra weapon. Let's put all the lessons you've given me shooting out at the ranch to good use. I'll either stay here and defend myself or be right behind you when you go inside the house."

Leon crossed to the trunk, opened it and tossed an extra Kevlar vest to Tanner. "We've got to move."

Tanner didn't like it but he was completely out of time and options. He slipped the Kevlar vest over Bree's head and strapped it tight, then reached for the weapon at his ankle and handed it to her. "Just like we practiced at home. And if anybody comes at you, you don't hesitate to pull the trigger. In the meantime, you stay right on my ass."

She actually smiled. "Nowhere I'd rather be."

They jogged toward the house. "You guys head around back," Leon told them. "Text me when you're in place. I'm going to go in hard through the front door. This place isn't very big, but maybe it has some sort of secret hidey-hole like Elliot's."

An alarm went off on Leon's watch. "That's it. We're at zero hour. She'll be underwater any second now."

Tanner shook his head. "Then I say we breach

the front door. Getting to the victim is more important than catching the perp if she decides to flee."

The two men nodded at each other and Tanner grabbed Bree's hand, pulling her right behind him.

"On your ass. I got it."

At the door, Leon turned to them. "Ready?"

Tanner nodded. "Let's do this."

Leon counted it down and kicked the door in. Bree kept one hand at his waist, under his vest so he'd know where she was. Both he and Leon kept their weapons raised, announcing their presence and moving quickly through the small house.

It didn't take long to realize there was no one here.

"There has to be some sort of secret room like you said." Leon was already looking around the closet, but nothing about it suggested that there was any sort of extra space.

"Bree," Tanner said. "Are you sure this is the place?"

"I'm positive this is where she was when she got into the chat room I set up. But there's no guarantee this is where the fourth victim is."

"You guys," Leon called out. "There's a shed out back. It's small, but it could possibly be our spot."

They rushed out the back door to the shed.

Tanner immediately pushed against the door but it only moved about a foot before getting stuck.

They all three looked down and saw the blood leaking out from under the door.

Tanner glanced at Leon and they both jammed their shoulders as hard as they could into the door. It finally moved enough for Tanner to slip inside.

He immediately saw what was blocking their entrance.

A woman's body.

Tanner pulled the body away from the door so Leon and Bree could enter behind him. A wall had been raised inside the shed, creating a narrow hallway. He felt the wrist of the woman on the ground.

"No pulse." As soon as he flipped her over, he saw why she didn't have a pulse.

She'd shot herself in the head. The gun was still in her hand.

"We got a body. Looks like a suicide."

Leon nodded and moved farther inside the shed, weapon still raised.

They all heard a strangled scream from behind the wall. Tanner dropped the dead woman's wrist and both he and Leon sprinted toward the small door at the end of the hall, Bree right behind them.

Once inside they all immediately recognized

the scene from the footage. They'd found the fourth victim.

And the woman was drowning.

They all rushed over, Tanner scooping his hand under the woman's head to help her sit up as far as possible, Bree and Leon using their arms to splash out water as quickly as they could in huge strokes.

When the woman finally coughed out the water she'd swallowed and was able to take a breath, they all relaxed a little bit, although Bree and Leon kept shoveling the water out. Tanner reached in his pocket and grabbed his phone, calling 9-1-1 to let them know they needed an ambulance at this address. Then he took over shoveling water so Leon could call Penelope and give an update.

Bree was talking to the woman, wiping her hair back from her face, reassuring her it was going to be okay. It was Betty Neighbors, the woman from Waco.

He met Bree's eyes over Betty's face. Bree had done it. She'd done the impossible: saved all four victims.

Chapter Twenty

As soon as the paramedics and uniformed officers showed up and took over to help Leon, Tanner got Bree out of there. They had done their part. Bree had very definitely done hers, even under the most trying of circumstances.

Suspect four, Kelly Braun, had killed herself. Maybe she'd realized there was no way she wouldn't be going to jail or was distraught to have been used by Rory Gresham. They were all just thankful she'd sent that one last message in the private chat room Bree could trace or they never would've found Betty Neighbors in time.

The rest of the case would be handled by Penelope and Leon. Bree and Tanner might have to come back and testify for the trials, but the work was done for them.

By the time the rest of the team arrived, Bree was swaying on her feet. Now that the action was over, her body was shutting down. Tanner let Leon know he was leaving and immediately took Bree back to the hotel.

She was asleep as soon as her head hit the pillow.

Tanner got them booked on a flight home for much later that evening. He wanted to get her out of here, back to Risk Peak where she belonged—where they *both* belonged—but had something he needed to do first.

Check on Michael Jeter himself. See for himself that it was, in fact, Jeter in that hospital. Make sure everyone surrounding him was truly aware of the danger he posed, not just to Bree but the world in general. Even injured, he was dangerous.

Tanner needed to see Jeter with his own eyes. He'd been there when Jeter had been arrested, but things between Tanner and Bree had been tentative then.

They weren't tentative now. Tanner was about to ask Bree to marry him. To be his forever.

He looked down at her asleep next to him from where he sat on the bed. He stood and walked over to his jacket and took out his mom's ring. Soon to be Bree's ring. He slid open the box and looked at it.

It didn't belong in his pocket anymore. It belonged on her finger. Noah had been right all along, he'd been overthinking it. The important part wasn't in the how or where Tanner asked her to be his bride, not for Bree.

The important part was that she understood that there was nothing in this world that could tear him away from her. That no matter what decisions they had to make—they would figure it out.

Together.

Michael Jeter also needed to understand that. That Bree was no longer alone. Would no longer need to run. Would no longer face any challenges that came her way with no backup.

Tanner would be right there standing between her and whatever danger thought it could get to her. So if Jeter had something planned, he should be aware of that.

Tanner had already put a text into Whitaker. He was going to hang out with Bree at the station in a few hours, so Tanner could go to Parkland Hospital. He wasn't trying to keep his meeting with Jeter a secret, but neither did he want Bree to feel like she needed to come with him.

He closed the ring box and slipped it back into his jacket pocket. He knew he wasn't going to ask her to marry him in a hotel in the middle of Dallas when they were both exhausted.

He lay back down on the bed beside her. She didn't stir as he pulled her into his arms, just fit against him the way their bodies had learned to do instinctively.

As soon as he got her back onto the ranch, he'd be down on one knee.

A few hours later Tanner awoke to Bree's bright smile. After spending an hour giving them both even more reason to smile, they packed up and headed to the station.

Bree was excited to be going home, but was more than happy to make sure Penelope understood the details of what she'd done to help stop the killers. Detailed reports would help make prosecuting the case that much easier.

Penelope and Leon were both looking a lot more relaxed, although Tanner doubted either of them had gotten a chance for much rest yet. But just knowing the worst was over was enough for now.

Whitaker walked up to shake Tanner's hand as he entered control central—now being returned to just a normal set of conference rooms—to a scattering of applause for Bree, which did nothing but make her embarrassed.

Jeremy was back and immediately had questions for Bree. She was obviously glad to have someone who understood and could appreciate what she'd done with the case, since she immediately turned and walked to the terminal with Jeremy without a word to Tanner or Whitaker.

Both men let out a chuckle. The behavior was so typically Bree that neither of them could be offended. The woman had a one-track mind. That had just saved four people's lives, so no point getting bent out of shape about it now.

"I called Sheriff Duggan and let her know we'd be on our way home today. Thankfully all has been quiet on the home front," Tanner said to Whitaker. "I know you like this sort of big-city action, but I think I'll stick with Risk Peak and our small-town stuff."

The other man clasped him on the shoulder. "Me too, brother. I'm glad we could help out here, but I think I'll stick with small town too. Although, we've had our share of action over the last few months."

That was the damn truth. "Hopefully we can have some excitement of a different type from here on out."

Whitaker raised an eyebrow. "Oh, yeah? Got something in mind?"

Tanner grinned. "Seems like wedding planning could be dangerous enough. I just need to get that woman home and out of danger long enough to ask her."

"A feat in and of itself." He chuckled and held out his hand to shake. "Congratulations. I knew you two were perfect for each other from the moment I tried to arrest you both for murder."

Now Tanner chuckled. "I'm just glad that didn't stick. Thank you for keeping an eye on Bree today. I just want to double-check on the Jeter situation myself while I'm in town."

"Are you sure you don't want me to come with you? I think it would take more guts than even Jeter has to try to get to Bree in the middle of a police station."

Tanner shook his head. "But if anyone would try, it's him. I won't take a chance with her safety. You're the only one I can trust to take this threat seriously. Until we know for sure Jeter is firmly locked away in prison, I consider him an outright threat to Bree."

"I'll be sure she's safe. But you watch your back too. Jeter is not just a danger to her."

Tanner would much rather him be a target than Bree, but he knew the truth. Bree was Jeter's obsession. Especially now after she'd put him in prison. Tanner was of no interest to the other man.

Bree was still deep in conversation with Jeremy, so Tanner said his goodbyes to Whitaker and headed to the hospital.

He wasn't able to get any information about Jeter at the hospital front desk, even after showing his badge. That was actually a good thing. It meant someone was doing their job right. Finally, Tanner asked for a representative from the US

Marshals, the law enforcement group in charge of transferring prisoners, to meet him there at the front desk. He had to wait nearly fifteen minutes before a man in his early fifties, hair cut short, with a hard, cynical look in his dark eyes finally approached him.

"You the fellow looking for information about Michael Jeter?" the man asked, fingers never far from the holster at his waist.

Tanner gave him a brief nod and slowly reached for his badge. "I'm Deputy Captain Tanner Dempsey out of Grand County, Colorado."

The man's eyes narrowed slightly. "You're one of the arresting officers in the Jeter case."

Tanner nodded. "That's right. I'm a little surprised you know that."

"When I found out it was Michael Jeter my men and I were responsible for guarding, I made it my business to know. I'm Aaron Pinfield." The man held out his hand and Tanner shook it. "You're a long way from home, Deputy Dempsey."

"Tanner, please. I was in town with my friend Bree Daniels, consulting on a completely separate case."

Pinfield nodded again. "Bree Daniels is in Dallas? That's an interesting coincidence. I read a lot about her too."

"Then you can understand why it was important to me to come over here myself and check out the situation. Jeter has a lot of powerful friends. Or did. We're not entirely certain exactly who or what he has left now."

"But no matter who it might be, Jeter is much less secure in this hospital than he would be in a prison." Pinfield finished for Tanner.

Tanner nodded, relieved the older man not only shared Tanner's concerns, but wasn't offended or threatened by them. "Bree Daniels has suffered a lot at Jeter's hands. Much more than what is written in any report. I have no doubt he is still obsessed with her and will do anything to get her back under his control."

Pinfield gave Tanner a solemn nod. "Well, that's just one more reason to make sure we don't let him out of our sight."

"I'd like to talk to Jeter. I'm taking Bree back to Colorado later this evening. I'd like to be able to tell her I saw Jeter with my own eyes. Reassure her a little bit."

Pinfield raised an eyebrow. "And I'm sure you might have a couple of things you'd like to say to the man while you've got eyes on him."

Tanner shifted a little bit, uncomfortable. Yeah, he damn well definitely had things he wanted to say to Jeter concerning Bree. "I'm not trying to disrupt your operation in any way—"

Pinfield held out a hand. "I'm not going to stop you from saying anything you have to say.

If that bastard had hurt my woman, I'd also want to make sure he understood that wouldn't be happening again."

Pinfield pointed down the hall and they began walking. "Well, I can get you in the door to give your message, but the truth is Jeter is not in much shape to hear anything. The burns on his face, neck and chest are pretty severe. We've been told by the doctors that this will be a long-term assignment. They expect Jeter to need all sorts of skin grafts and surgeries."

Tanner winced. "No offense to you or your team, but that's not the news I wanted. The longer Jeter is out in the open, the more people involved with his recovery, the more of a chance there is somebody working to break him out."

"No argument here. But we are aware of the situation and we're going to be on top of it the entire time."

"I would consider it a personal favor if you would keep me posted concerning any changes or concerns you have. I have friends in law enforcement throughout the country, both state and federal. We are willing to help out any way we can."

Pinfield reached up and squeezed Tanner's shoulder. "Don't worry. I'm committed to making sure that man spends the rest of his life in prison. That bastard lying in that hospital bed is not going anywhere. I'm going to make damn sure of it." He then stopped outside the door that had two guards stationed at it.

Tanner nodded and reached for the door. "Thank you."

"Thank you for getting Jeter here in the first place. I'll give you a few minutes to say your piece. Like I said, I don't think he can hear you. But everything in this room is recorded anyway, so I'd be more than happy to play it back for him later."

Tanner walked into the room and closed the door behind him. Immediately he could see why Pinfield had warned him that Jeter wouldn't be providing Tanner any sort of discussion.

The man lying in the bed was barely alive. He had so many tubes and monitors attached to his body it was almost impossible to notice the restraints that kept both wrists attached to the bed. Honestly, the cuffs seemed like overkill. The idea that Jeter could inflict harm on others was almost ludicrous. In this state he didn't look like he could even get out of bed.

Tanner reached into his pocket and pulled out the small fingerprinting kit. Greg Lightfoot said he had watched the officers do it, but Tanner couldn't see any harm in doing it himself to be sure.

It took him less than a minute to manipulate the fingers of the unconscious Jeter into the formation he needed to get the prints. And less than another minute after that to be comparing them to the set he'd brought with him. He even used a magnifying glass.

It was definitely a match.

Tanner wiped off Jeter's fingertips and folded the set of prints he'd taken and put it in his back pocket. Maybe they would reassure Bree. In some ways he wished he'd brought her. Seeing Jeter like this—so hopeless and pathetic—might help heal something in her.

Jeter let out a groan like somehow even under all the drugs he was still in pain.

However much pain he was in, it wasn't enough.

"Did you ever give her anything when she was in pain, you son of a bitch? When you broke her bones or cut her or didn't let her sleep for days at a time?"

Jeter didn't answer. Tanner hadn't expected him to. "I hope part of you can hear me, although I'll still get Pinfield to deliver the message later just to make sure. Bree—Bethany—she's not yours anymore. She'll never be yours."

Tanner's hands balled into fists. "She's not alone and she'll never be alone again. If you want her, you'll have to go through me. And that's not happening. So I hope you live a nice long life in your prison cell. Not for what you did as a terrorist, but for what you did to her."

He stared at Jeter's unconscious form for a long minute.

There was more he wanted to say but he realized that he'd rather get back to Bree and start their future than spend time here fighting ghosts of the past.

"I'm going to ask her to marry me," Tanner whispered. "I've got the ring right here. She will never be alone and defenseless again. So remember that if you decide you're coming for her. People have her back now."

He turned and walked out the door. Pinfield was still standing outside.

"Say everything you needed to say?"

"Yep. I suppose I should feel bad about what shape he's in. But I don't, not even the smallest bit."

"I assume you fingerprinted him with that kit you had in your pocket?"

Tanner raised an eyebrow. "You don't miss much."

"That would be why I am a US Marshal. And also, this." Pinfield pulled out a file and handed it to Tanner. He opened it and found multiple sets of fingerprints, which had been taken by hand and run against a master set that was attached to the inside of the folder.

"We take fingerprints at the beginning of every shift, after any sort of medical procedure where Jeter is taken out of this room, or if anybody just gets the heebie-jeebies. We're all aware that the first thing someone trying to assist Jeter would do is change his fingerprints in the system. So we always use the hard copy. Those fingerprints have not changed since that prison bus accident. And we're going to make sure no one tries to switch them out under our watch."

Tanner shook the man's hand. "Thank you. Thank you for taking this seriously. Thank you for making it so that I can sleep a little better at night."

Pinfield smiled. "Just doing my job."

Tanner left the hospital feeling much better than he had when he'd arrived. He shot a text to Whitaker letting him know that he was on his way back.

Pinfield had this under control. Tanner wasn't sure there was anything he would be doing differently if he was in charge.

But more important, it was good news for Bree. Soon Jeter would be in prison where he belonged.

He opened his car door and got inside. They still had a few hours before their flight. Maybe he would see if Bree wanted to come back here. She hadn't gotten her closure on the stand like she wanted. Maybe this could be the next best thing.

He was about to pull out of his parking spot when a knock on his window stopped him. All Tanner could see were the scrubs of a doctor. He rolled down his window a little.

"Can I help you?"

"I'm sorry. I'm Dr. Arnold. Are you Tanner Dempsey? Deputy Tanner Dempsey?"

Tanner rolled his window the rest of the way down. "I am. Is everything okay?"

"Oh, yes. I just wanted to see…"

The doctor shifted and Tanner felt a sharp pinch at the side of his back. He was reaching for his weapon as everything began to blur.

The doctor leaned down so that he was now gazing directly into Tanner's window and Tanner could see his face.

"You…" His voice sounded distant and foreign to his own ears. The fingers reaching for his sidearm wouldn't seem to work.

"What were you just saying about how if I wanted to get to Bree I was going to need to go through you?"

Michael Jeter's face without any burns at all smiled out at Tanner.

And then everything faded to black.

Chapter Twenty-One

Tanner knew he was in trouble as soon as he woke up. He was in a box, not unlike the ones Rory Gresham and his cronies had used on their victims.

But this one was wood. Basically a plain coffin, just not yet closed.

"Don't worry, Tanner. I can call you Tanner, right? Deputy Captain Dempsey seems so formal." Jeter waved from a few feet away. "Either way, don't worry, I'm not going to drown you. You had enough drowning excitement for one week, right? Plus, who has time to figure out all those details about how many drips of water it will take. That's just nuts."

Tanner blinked, trying to clear his mind. "Who is that man in the hospital and how does he have your fingerprints?"

How was it possible that Jeter was standing here right now without a scratch on him?

Tanner's hands were tied at the wrists and

resting on his chest. He tried to move his legs but they were restrained also inside this casket-shaped box.

"I'm going to be honest with you, and this might make you think I'm a bad person, but I honestly don't know the name of the guy in the hospital. Believe it or not, I've been prepared for something of this measure to occur for the last ten years. That man lived a wonderful life of luxury and all he had to do was be roughly my same height and build, have the same blood type as me and have his fingerprints removed and mine lasered onto his fingers."

"He's your double."

"Yes, exactly! But honestly, I didn't even come up with the idea myself. You'd be surprised at how many political leaders have doubles in case their death is the only option for escaping a situation, and yet they don't actually want to die."

Tanner shook his head, still trying to shake away some of the cobwebs. This couldn't be happening.

"I know, right?" Jeter said. "It's all such cloak-and-dagger craziness. Hard to believe it's true."

"So you've been planning this from the beginning," Tanner said. He kept his eyes on Jeter but glanced up behind him and around whenever he could. "I can't believe you don't have a whole army here."

Jeter threw his arms up. "I have been around people—so many damn people—every day for months. I needed time alone for a while. But don't worry—I still have my loyal followers I'll band together eventually."

Tanner followed Jeter with his eyes as the man walked around. Why did this place look familiar?

"Between you and me, I'm not cut out for prison. The man taking my place will do much better, plus his family will live in complete luxury for the rest of their existence. But me? I have other, better things to do than sit in a cell every day. I need to be able to move around. Some people aren't meant to do nothing, you know what I mean, Tanner? I can't be someone who does *nothing*."

"Why didn't you just kill me in the parking lot?"

"Why, Bree, of course. My Bethany. You are the only way I can get her to come to me of her own accord. If I didn't use you, she would go to ground, hide. And we both know how good she is at that."

"Do you expect me to just call her and lead her here to slaughter? I'll die first."

Jeter actually winked at him. "Don't worry—you're going to die anyway. I mean, hell, Deputy, you said so in that hospital room. If I wanted her, I had to go through you."

"You were listening in the hospital room?"

Jeter rolled his eyes. "I feel like all I've been doing for the past twenty-four hours is listening. Listening in the hospital room. Listening to your investigation."

"What?"

"Oh, come on. I even helped you with the last one. Bethany got a little sloppy making that shell program to trace the chat room. Your suspect wasn't going to fall for it. And that woman in the box was going to die. I stepped in, shot the suspect in the head and sent you a little message. I would think you'd be a little more grateful for that."

Jeter had been a step ahead of them this whole time, waiting for the right moment to strike against Bree.

Tanner shifted slightly and finally realized why this place seemed so familiar. They were inside the restaurant where Shelby's body had been found. One of the first places Whitaker had shown him when he and Bree got here—in his old neighborhood.

"You've been inside the police files," Tanner said. "Otherwise you would've never known about this place."

He shrugged. "I've just wanted to be close to Bethany, and this case has been her sole focus the last couple of days. She's really just so wonderful, isn't she? Her brain. I want to say it's the sexiest thing about her, but now that she's all grown up I can't say that anymore."

Tanner began to fight against his restraints.

"Come on now, Tanner. You're about to be her fiancé, right? You can't tell me you don't think she's sexy."

Jeter began tossing something casually in his hand. It didn't take Tanner long to realize it was the ring box.

"You stay away from her, Jeter. Just disappear and leave her alone. I'm not going to let you take her."

Jeter tilted his head to the side with a condescending smile. "Like I said, you're not going to be alive to have a say-so. Your case has actually been pretty helpful to me overall."

Tanner stopped his struggles. There was no way out of this box the way he was restrained. He needed to work smarter, not harder.

And do it before Jeter got Bree here.

"How did the case help you? Besides getting us to Dallas."

"I have to admit, that was quite fortuitous. I thought I was going to need to travel all the way to Colorado before seeing Bethany. But instead, the case brought her here. But it did so much more than that."

Tanner felt the slightest give in the zip tie

around his wrist. Would it be possible to work his hand out? He could feel his backup weapon still in his ankle holster, but had no way to get to it, restrained like this.

"Once I hacked into the Dallas PD system, I was able to see everything you all—and Bethany—were seeing. She was so busy trying to figure out how to follow the broadcasts, she didn't even try to fortify her computer actions against possible outsiders. So I was able to know exactly where Bethany was and what she was doing every minute. It was quite refreshing, I tell you, to be following someone as brilliant as her."

Tanner let Jeter continue to monologue. Anything to buy him time to try to get his wrist loose.

"Plus, your case provided me with the ketamine I needed to knock you unconscious. And most important, it made me realize how I could get Bethany's attention."

"I thought you said you weren't going to drown me." Tanner kept trying to twist his wrist to loosen the zip tie but it wasn't working.

"No." Jeter asked, "Who has time for that sort of drama? No, I have a much better plan. I'm going to suffocate you."

Suddenly the box Tanner was in seemed much smaller.

"I'll add a little carbon monoxide to make sure the job is well and truly done, thus our stay at a restaurant—but yeah. I thought suffocating you would get Bethany here pretty damn quickly."

"Bree is too smart to show up here just because you threaten her."

"Well, that's where the case comes in once again… How about some live footage of you dying? That'll be pretty damn motivating for our girl, don't you think?"

"You really are brilliant," Jeremy said as Bree finished showing him everything she'd done to track the killers. "I can't believe you wrote that shell program to track number four in under ninety seconds."

Bree shook her head. "Honestly, I can't believe she fell for it. Obviously she must have been really upset or she would've quickly realized it was a trap."

Of course, obviously she'd been really upset since she killed herself.

"Thank God it worked," Jeremy muttered. "After all that, I can't believe none of the victims died."

"Except the first two," Bree reminded him. "The ones that were never broadcast."

"Penelope is concentrating on Rory Gresham for those two, since he was the ringleader. Looks like he was practicing on them. Making sure it would all work before he brought the others in."

Bree stretched her back. "I hope she can get a confession out of him."

Jeremy smiled and stood up. "If anyone can, it's Penelope. And if she can't, he'll still be going away for a long time. At least four counts of conspiracy to commit murder."

"I hope that's a long time."

Jeremy patted her shoulder with his nonburned hand. "I'm sorry I was a jerk to you before. If it wasn't for you, all four of those women would be dead."

She shrugged. "I got lucky for some of it."

"Yeah, well, your luck is still based in skill. So just take the compliment. I hope we'll get to work together again, Bree."

Bree looked around after Jeremy went over to talk to Penelope, searching for Tanner. She hadn't seen him since she'd started talking to Jeremy and that had to have been twenty or thirty... She looked at her phone. Crap. Make that two hours ago.

Maybe he'd gotten tired of waiting for her to finish with Jeremy and decided to grab some lunch or something.

"You looking for Tanner?" Whitaker walked over to her.

"Yeah. I had no idea Jeremy and I had been discussing my methods for two hours. Where'd Tanner go?"

"Um, he had some things he wanted to look into with the case."

"Is there a problem? Oh, no, there aren't more victims or anything, right?" The thought that she might have missed something ate at her.

"Oh, no, nothing like that. Actually I think this had to do with another case."

"What other case?"

Whitaker looked down at his phone. "Look, you haven't heard from Tanner? He texted me over an hour ago. He should be back here any second. I'm sure he'll explain everything then."

Bree's eyes narrowed. "What would he need to explain, Richard? Where is he?"

Whitaker shifted on his feet. "I think it's better if you hear it from him. I'm sure he'll—"

Bree's phone chirped in her hand. She looked down and saw a text from Tanner. She shooed Whitaker away with her hand. "You're off the hook, poker face. I'll get him to tell me what's going on."

"Good," Whitaker muttered, and took off in a hurry.

I need something from you.

Bree's brows furrowed at the message. Tanner usually started texts with a greeting when they hadn't been around each other. She shot back one of her own.

Everything okay? What do you need?

I need you to sit down at the air gap system and make sure no one is paying attention to you.

Bree froze and stared down at the phone in her hand. If she'd had to have guessed she would've said that Tanner wouldn't even have known what an air gap computer system was, much less that they had one here. It was an internal system, not connected to the internet.

Are you there?

The terse words had her moving quickly to the terminal. Tanner needed something from her and if she could give it, she would. She could ask questions later.

A few seconds later she was in front of the system, using the DOS operating function to get to a workable spot on the computer. She typed back on her phone.

Okay, I'm on. What do you need?

She waited, but nothing came back up on her

phone. Finally a near-silent beep on the computer itself got her attention.

And two tiny words.

Hello, Bethany.

Chapter Twenty-Two

Bree stared at the screen. How was Jeter contacting her through this system? It was a closed system, not utilized for communication outside of the Dallas law enforcement department.

Had Jeter somehow found a way to hack into their system from the hospital? She thought he was still unconscious, but obviously not.

Her cell phone buzzed in her hand, a video call from Tanner. She needed to let him know that Jeter was somehow in the law enforcement system. God only knew what he could do from there.

She was still staring at the computer screen when she pressed the receive button for Tanner's call. Was there any way to trace Jeter through the air gap system?

"Tanner, we've got a problem. Jeter has somehow—"

Her stomach dropped as she finally looked away from the computer and at the screen of her phone. It wasn't Tanner's brown eyes looking back at her. It was the face from her nightmares.

She stared at the picture in silence, unable to even force any words past her throat that seemed suddenly completely closed. If she could figure out anything to say anyway.

Why did Jeter have Tanner's phone?

The computer screen beeped softly in front of her.

Put in headphones. If you're interested in seeing Deputy Dempsey again alive.

Bree couldn't stop the small cry that escaped her. She reached down into her bag and pulled out the headphones, placing them in her ears.

"Bethany, you look well," Jeter said. "It's so good to see you. I chose this computer for a reason. I want you to set your phone against the screen and keep your hands resting on the front of the keyboard, but not typing anything. This way I can see you and your hands, and I can hear you."

"What do you want?" she said softly.

"Right at this moment I want to make sure nobody knows that you're talking to me. So I'm going to turn off the video feed on my end—" the phone screen went black "—but I can still see and hear you. Now, put the phone where I said and your hands on the keyboard. I know what you're capable of, and we'll not have any of that."

She did as he asked.

"Good. That's very good, Bethany."

Bile curdled in her gut and her fingers began to shake. This was just like when she'd been a child. He'd always been behind her back, looking over her shoulder, where she couldn't see him. All she'd ever been able to do was hear his voice.

"How do you have Tanner's phone?" she finally got out.

"He lent it to me."

"I find that hard to believe." The best possible scenario would be that Jeter had somehow stolen Tanner's phone without him being aware of it. The worst... Bree couldn't even stand to think about the worst.

"How about you just ask him yourself."

Tension flooded her body. "What?"

Instead of a picture on her phone, a small video box opened on the computer screen.

It was Tanner, lying in a box—a casket. His hands were bound and crossed on his chest. He had a gag in his mouth.

Bree couldn't hold back the little sob that escaped her.

"Quiet now, Bethany. If you let anyone know you're talking to me, you're going to watch your boyfriend die pretty brutally. After all, he's already in a casket. Makes cleanup pretty easy."

"You son of a—"

Bree's words were cut off as Whitaker walked up to her. Instantly the video box containing Tanner disappeared from the screen.

"Everything okay?" Whitaker asked.

Bree's fingers grasped the end of the keyboard hard. Jeter was watching. If she moved to warn Whitaker she had no doubt Tanner was a dead man.

"Yeah. Just wrapping things up. Ready to get home—you know how it is."

"What did Tanner say when he called?"

Bree swallowed hard, struggling not to give herself away. "Not much. That he would be back soon and we would talk."

Think. She had to figure out a way to let Whitaker or someone know Jeter had Tanner.

"All right. I'll let you finish up here. I'm not going to fly back to Risk Peak for another couple of days. Just want to make sure Penelope doesn't need any further help."

"I'm sure she appreciates that."

Whitaker gave her a smile and walked off. Bree wanted to scream out for him to come back.

"See, you handled that quite well." Jeter's voice came back on in her ear. The picture popped back on the computer screen. "Now maybe if you continue to follow directions so well, your Tanner will live to see another day."

It was all she could do to stop herself from reaching up and touching the screen. Touching Tanner. As if her touch could somehow make this all go away.

"It's like the case you've been working, isn't it? I've been watching. I can't help but be proud of what you did there. Helping arrest Gresham, Elliot the others. Those people were reasonably adept. The Dallas Police Department would've never caught them without your help. The women in the boxes would be dead."

"Were you a part of all this?" Bree didn't know how it was possible, but if it was, Jeter would be the one to accomplish it.

"Oh, no. I can't take credit for that. But it did make it very easy and convenient to follow you the last day."

She was sure it had been. She'd been trying to work as fast as possible, only hiding herself from the killers. She'd never dreamed somebody would backdoor their way into what she was already backdooring into.

"But the prison bus accident. You orchestrated that." She already knew it was the truth, she didn't have to ask it as a question.

"Come on now, Bethany. You had to have

known I would get out. You've always known I would come for you."

Bree shut her eyes. He was right. She hadn't wanted to admit it, even to herself, but she'd always known Jeter was going to find a way to come after her.

She'd let herself become so soft. Someone her mother—who had given her life trying to protect Bree and teach her how to best combat the dangers posed by Jeter and the Organization—wouldn't even recognize now.

Bree had let herself fall prey to the magic of her and Tanner's love. Like that was some sort of protection. As if it was some sort of talisman able to protect them from the reality of the evil of the Organization.

She'd let herself believe that the law would be able to control Jeter, someone who'd fooled the entire world for decades.

She should've known better.

She studied the video of Tanner on the screen once again. He didn't look panicked. The only way someone would even know that he was scared at all—and he had to be, sitting inside a casket with a madman standing over him—was by the frantic movement of his finger against his chest.

"I'm sorry," she whispered.

She should've never allowed herself to stop

permanently in Risk Peak. She'd brought this danger straight to Tanner.

"Why all the theatrics?" she finally asked Jeter. "Are you trying to outdrama the case we just worked on?"

"Don't worry I'm not going to drown Tanner, not when suffocation will work just fine. Or if we need to speed things up, I've always got some carbon monoxide."

Bree swallowed another sob, looking at Tanner again.

His finger was still moving in overtime. She wanted to reach out and grab it, just to calm it. To…

His finger was moving in a pattern.

Bree fought to keep her face neutral. To keep this news away from Jeter.

What are you trying to tell me, hot lips?

Because he definitely was.

Tanner must know where he was. Why would Jeter gag Tanner? It was just as much overkill as using the voice modulator.

She watched his fingers more carefully. Yes. He was using Morse code.

W-H-I-T. Pause. *S-H-E-L-B-Y.* Pause. *S-C-E-N-E.*

The message repeated from there. When they'd first gotten here, Whitaker had taken Tanner to the crime scene where the girl from his neighborhood had been found. Where was that? Bree wasn't completely sure, but knew it was somewhere on the south side of town.

If Jeter had hacked the Dallas PD system, he would definitely have knowledge of that location.

The question was, how did Bree let anyone else know where Tanner was without alerting Jeter.

"What do you want, Jeter?"

"I want a lot of things. I want you to not have run away a dozen years ago. I want you to have not betrayed me a few months ago. But for right now, I'll settle for you trading yourself for Tanner's life."

She would do it. She would do it in a heartbeat, every single time. She would give herself over to Jeter a thousand times if it meant Tanner lived.

"Fine. I'll do it. I—"

Before she could say anything else, Penelope walked over and stopped directly in front of Bree's computer station. "Everything okay? Where's Tanner?"

Jeter's voice came on in her ear as the picture disappeared once again from the computer screen. "Get rid of her, Bethany. We'll go ahead and close the casket so Tanner can get a taste of what it might feel like in a few minutes if you don't cooperate."

"Um…" Bree looked up at Penelope trying not to sweat. "You'll have to ask Whitaker. They were hanging out together last time I saw them. I'm sure Tanner's around here somewhere."

Penelope's eyes narrowed. She glanced down at Bree's hands then back up to her face.

The woman suspected something, or was at least noticing something was off. Bree could do nothing to warn the other woman. If Penelope said the wrong thing it would cost Tanner his life.

"Well, I just wanted to come by and say thank you for all the work you did with the case. We wouldn't have been able to get those women out, without you."

Bree gave a little nod. This was the last time she was going to be able to signal to anyone that Tanner was in trouble. How could she do it?

"I'm glad I could help."

Penelope was still studying her. "And I'm really glad that you and I got to spend some time together and get to know each other so well. All the one-on-one time we spent together."

Bree kept her face completely neutral. She and Penelope very definitely had not gotten to know each other. Bree had forgotten the woman's name more than once.

"Um, yeah. That was nice."

"You listening to music like you always do when you're working?" Penelope continued.

"Get rid of her, *now*, Bethany."

"Yeah. Music. You know how I love music when I'm working." Bree nodded.

"You'll be sure to get me that footage you set up before you leave, right? The special recordings you set up? Sorry we were so hard on you about that. I guess even I get territorial sometimes when it comes to cases."

The monitor footage. Yes, it would still be running even now. If Penelope checked it she would be able to see what Jeter was sending her right now.

And even better, Jeter had no idea it existed since Bree didn't use an official Dallas PD system.

"Yes." Bree nodded enthusiastically. "You will very definitely want to look through that for the case. Jeremy knows how to access it. You'll want to do that first thing. Thanks, Penelope."

Penelope nodded and said a fast goodbye.

Bree prayed the woman had understood exactly what she meant and was checking to get the necessary screenshots right now.

"She's gone. Where do you want me to meet you?"

Jeter rattled off an address and Bree knew right away it wasn't where he was holding Tanner. It was nowhere near Whitaker's old neighborhood.

"That's where Tanner is? And if I come there and agree to stay with you, you'll let him go?"

"That's the deal. He'll be right here beside me. And the moment you agree to go away with me, you can send a message to one of your little cop friends and have them come rescue our Tanner. If everyone moves quickly enough, maybe Tanner will get out of this before he suffocates. You have my word."

Bree barely refrained from rolling her eyes. Jeter had no intention of letting Tanner out of that casket alive.

"Put the picture back on. I want to see him one more time. If I go away with you this will be the last time I'll ever be able to."

She needed to make sure Penelope got the message about where Tanner was. Saw that it was his fingers moving.

Jeter put the video of Tanner back up on the screen. Bree bit back a sob as Jeter had to pry open the casket cover in order for her to be able to see him. Sweat was running off his forehead and his eyes were a lot more apprehensive now.

His finger still kept beating the same Morse code pattern. Tanner knew he was in trouble, but was not panicking.

Bree brought her fingers up to her mouth and kissed them and then placed them on the screen. Hopefully to Jeter it would look like she was saying goodbye to Tanner. But once she got her fingers to the screen, where she was out of Jeter's view, she pointed to Tanner's finger tapping the code. She pointed three times, praying it would be enough.

They had to get to Tanner.

"Fine, I'm coming. Leave the casket open. I can meet you at that address in fifteen minutes."

"I don't think so. I think the casket being closed gives you more incentive to move more quickly. How long do you think it takes for someone to suffocate in a casket? An hour? Thirty minutes? I bet you'd like to Google that, wouldn't you, but you can't because you're going to leave your phone on video with me the whole time. If at any point I can't see your hands or I think you're trying to warn someone about what's going on, your boyfriend dies."

Bree got up, keeping the phone so Jeter could see what she was doing. She was going to need to get a car. She knew how to steal one, but doing it in a police department parking lot was not the best of circumstances. But what other choice did she have?

She was almost to the door when Whitaker's voice called out.

"Bree, where you going?"

She grimaced and turned back to him, keeping the phone at an awkward angle where Jeter could still see everything.

"I, uh, just needed some fresh air. And thought

I might grab a bite to eat or something. I'll be back in just a few."

"I think you ought to wait until Tanner gets back. I don't think he would like for you to be wandering around by yourself even if Jeter is in the hospital."

How was she going to get out of here without making this a huge deal? "Yeah. But I—"

"Or I can come with you," Whitaker offered.

Damn it. She tightened her grip on the phone. "No I—"

"Hey, Whit, can I talk to you for a second?" Penelope walked up to them and placed a hand on Whitaker's shoulder.

"Sure. But—"

"This can't wait. It's about one of the victims."

Whitaker looked torn. "It's not a good idea for Bree to be going outside on her own."

Penelope studied Bree. "You still listening to your music?"

Bree touched her headphones. "Yeah. Helps me relax." The woman had to have remembered her earlier comment about how music distracted her.

"Here's the keys to my car. It's parked right out front. Go do what you need to do. We'll see you soon."

Bree turned and walked away, leaving Penel-

ope behind to calm the blustering Whitaker and
hopefully figure it all out.

Bree prayed it was enough.

Chapter Twenty-Three

Tanner watched from his definite disadvantage point as Jeter put the call on mute. He could see Bree's face, taut with worry, as she got up and made her way toward the door.

"Do you have something to say, Deputy?" Jeter pulled the gag out of Tanner's mouth.

"You're not going to get away with this."

Tanner wanted to say more. Wanted to say that Jeter was underestimating Bree once again. Wanted to say that she was smarter than he gave her credit for, and should learn his lesson since she'd bested him twice already.

But Tanner knew better than to interrupt his enemy when he was making a mistake.

"Actually, I think I *am* going to get away with it. Don't you see? Bethany is coming back to me. It didn't take much."

"She's coming back to you because she has a kind heart and didn't want to see me die."

Jeter sighed. "She always did tend to lean toward being too soft. I tried to correct that in her. Would have succeeded if she hadn't run away. But don't worry, I'll succeed now. I'm the one she was always meant to be with."

Jeter took out the ring box and began tossing it in the air again. "Honestly, Tanner. What could you give her? I am the one who always challenged her. I'm the one who helped her find the strength within herself."

"You tortured her and her mother, isolated her and made her life a living hell. Bree Daniels is a woman of exceptional strength and beauty despite you, not because of you."

Jeter's eyes narrowed. "Her name is *Bethany*. She may have forgotten it, but don't worry, by the time I'm finished with her she will never forget who she is or who she belongs to ever again."

Tanner looked at the phone showing Bree leaving the police station. Had she figured out his clues? Tanner had to believe she had. Because there was no way in hell Jeter was going to let Tanner go free.

Jeter stuffed the gag back in Tanner's mouth. "I don't think anybody's going to be around to hear you if you yell, but just in case. It's time for me to go meet our girl. Ironically, I'm meeting her at a place just a couple blocks from here. Someday I'll tell her how close she was to where you died. We'll have a good laugh about it."

Jeter rested his arms on the side of the casket and winked at Tanner. "See, I think there's something you don't really understand about Bethany. She can be molded. It might take a little more pressure than when she was a teenager, but I have no doubt I can do it."

Tanner fought down panic as Jeter began to close the lid. "And just in case I underestimated Bethany once more—because honestly, fool me three times then I'm just a damned idiot—know that I've made certain that if she doesn't choose me, she'll never choose anyone else ever again."

The lid of the coffin closed, and blackness surrounded him.

"Sorry it had to be this way, Tanner." Jeter's voice was distant through the thick wood of the casket. "But Bethany and I are meant to be together. It was always supposed to be this way."

Some sort of lock clicked on the outside and Tanner was trapped by the darkness and his own helplessness.

JETER ALLOWED BREE to pull up the GPS on Penelope's car, but made her turn the phone so that he could see exactly what she was doing. Smart. Because given two minutes, Bree could probably get a message sent to someone through the GPS. Of course, Jeter could do the same thing, which was why he'd circumvented that option.

Bree was a little surprised when the address he'd given her brought her to a popular lunchtime sandwich shop. She would not have thought that Jeter would show his face in public, given how well-known he now was.

"Park the car and take the white Honda Civic." A picture of a license plate filled her screen.

Bree did as she was directed. It was actually a smart move on Jeter's part. If Penelope tracked the GPS in her car, it would just show that Bree was at a restaurant like she'd said she would be.

Maybe Jeter really was bringing her to where he held Tanner and planned to let him go unharmed once Bree showed up.

But she knew better. The best she could hope for right now was that Tanner wasn't already dead. That Penelope and Whitaker figured out the clue and got to him in time.

"Okay, I'm in the new car. Where do you want me to go?"

An address popped up on the GPS of the car and Bree began following the directions. At least this time it was leading her closer to where Tanner had indicated he was being held.

"You're never going to be able to live a normal life, Michael. Too many people know you. There will be a reward out for your capture."

Jeter's face filled the screen once more. "Sadly, this face will have to go. You're right, it's much too noticeable. Yours will have to go too, Bethany, darling."

Bree drove the rest of the way in silence, gripping the steering wheel so hard her knuckles were white.

Was she really driving toward this madman who had made her life a living hell for so many years? And all for the possible but unlikely chance that Tanner was still alive?

She tried not to think about what Tanner would want her to do because she already knew.

Tanner would never want her to put herself back into Jeter's clutches. Not just because of the price she would pay personally, but because of what Jeter would accomplish once he eventually wore Bree's resistance down and she cracked.

Bree and Jeter working together unchecked would become an unstoppable force. Law enforcement would never be able to capture him again.

Tanner would definitely not want Bree to be giving herself to Jeter, even to save his life. If he could communicate with her right now he would tell her to turn the car around and drive the other way.

The only reason she didn't was because she knew the other side of that truth too.

If the roles were reversed and Tanner could put

himself in jeopardy for the chance that it might save her life, he would do it in a heartbeat.

That's what love was.

So she kept driving in the direction Jeter indicated.

A few minutes later she pulled up outside what looked like an old strip mall with adjoining shops. It might have been a thriving part of this neighborhood at one time, but had long been abandoned.

"Just come in through the pawnshop door," Jeter said in her ear.

Bree got out of the car and marched slowly toward the entrance. Each step got harder and harder, like a prisoner walking to execution.

It wasn't much of a metaphor if it was happening in reality.

She opened the door and walked inside. The interior of the building had been completely gutted. All the windows were blacked out, leaving the inside barren and completely dark.

Bree waited a few seconds for her eyes to adjust, then walked a little farther inside the building.

"That's right," Jeter said. "Just keep walking straight. You'll find my little office."

Bree used the light from the screen to guide her toward the only thing she could see inside the building besides boxes—a small room in the back corner.

It wasn't completely unlike the rooms that had been used to hold the kidnapped women.

"Let's go, Bethany. We don't have all day."

Bree gritted her teeth and reached for the doorknob, then pushed the door open. There stood the man she'd been running and hiding from half her life, smiling with his arms outstretched like they were old friends.

"I'm here." She shut the door behind her, but stayed close to it. "Now where's Tanner?"

Jeter gestured at one of the multiple monitors sitting around the room. There were at least half a dozen different computer systems, although Bree wasn't the least bit surprised. Jeter would always be surrounded by computers.

"Deputy Dempsey is right where I left him."

"We had a deal. I came here, and you let Tanner go."

Jeter just smiled. "It's so good to see you, Bethany. The last time we met, when you betrayed me, the circumstances weren't optimal. I've had a lot of time to think about you the last few months. About you and I and how we fit together."

He took a step closer as he continued. "About how we can't allow things to stand in our way even when methods might sometimes seem cruel. About ends justifying the means."

"You're not going to let Tanner go, are you? You never planned to let him go."

"Come over here and look at your Tanner."

Bree didn't want to move away from the door, but had no choice when Jeter picked up the gun on the table and pointed it at her.

"Come look." He gestured with the gun.

She wasn't going to move. She knew firsthand there was a lot worse he could do to her than to kill her quickly with a bullet. If Tanner was going to die anyway, then Bree wasn't going to subject herself to a life of horror with Jeter. Wasn't even going to subject herself to one single touch from him.

And then she saw just the slightest bit of movement on the monitor with Tanner. Something was happening over there, around the closed casket. Maybe Penelope had figured it out.

She had to keep Jeter distracted. Gritting her teeth, she took a step away from the door.

"There's a good girl."

"You know I'll hate you forever. For killing Tanner? I'll never forgive you."

Bree forced herself to hold completely still as Jeter closed the distance between them and reached over to touch a strand of her hair. "We both know I can break you," he whispered. "You'll be whatever I mold you into."

She glanced at the monitor again while Jeter

was obsessed with touching the side of her face. There was definitely something happening.

"But I'm not a complete monster. I've attached a canister of carbon monoxide to Tanner's casket. All I have to do is flip the switch and he'll die without any pain within seconds."

He stepped back from her a little and she knew he would be turning to the monitor. She couldn't allow that to happen. With a scream she pounced toward the table, sweeping her arms across it and dumping everything, including the monitor with the picture of Tanner's casket, onto the floor. Screeching, she dived for more of the computer equipment, ready to drag it off the table also. She kicked everything her feet came in contact with for good measure.

An arm wrapped around her waist and slung her back into the far corner of the room.

Bree was breathing hard, blood boiling. She'd never thrown a fit like this in her life and it actually felt a little good. But God, she hoped it was enough. For Penelope and Whitaker to get to Tanner and get him out.

But even if they did, they weren't going to be able to help her. They had no way of knowing where she was.

The best thing Bree could hope for might be to get Jeter to kill her here.

Jeter shook his head and made a tsking noise.

"I'm so disappointed in you, Bethany. Now your would've-been fiancé will die much more slowly and painfully, all so you could have a little temper tantrum."

"What?"

Jeter took a ring box off the table and began tossing it in the air.

"This. Your boyfriend has been carrying it around. Seems like our Tanner was planning on proposing."

He tossed the ring box to her and she caught it out of automatic reaction more than anything else. She opened it and tried to bite back her sob.

"Oops," he said. "I guess I spoiled the surprise. But since Tanner will be dead in a few minutes anyway, there's no real harm done."

Bree ignored him, reaching out to run her fingers over the ring. This had been Tanner's mom's engagement ring. Bree remembered it from when the older woman had shown her over dinner one night.

Had Tanner really been planning to ask her to marry him when she'd been afraid he was going to ask her to move out of the ranch house?

Jeter reached over and snatched the ring out of her hand. Bree bit back another cry.

"Please. You've taken Tanner. Just let me keep this."

Jeter tilted his head and studied her. "You really did have feelings for him, didn't you?"

Bree was surprised when he lifted her hand and placed the ring box back on her palm. "I will let you keep this. Because someday you will readily give it back to me. The way you just ran your fingers so lovingly over it will be how you rub them over the ring I give you instead."

Bree forced herself not to cringe. The important thing was that she had the ring.

Jeter crossed back over to the second table Bree hadn't knocked over. He picked up a syringe lying there and turned back to her.

"I got this from one of the kidnappers in your case. The same one I helped you catch. You didn't really think she was going to fall for that shell program did you?"

"Actually, no. I was pretty surprised when we got her message."

Jeter held up his arms. "That's because it was me. That lady in the bathtub thing would've definitely been dead by the time he found her, if I hadn't killed the kidnapper and sent a message to you. See, I'm not such a terrible guy."

Bree looked around the room. There's no way she was going to make it to the door without him catching her and injecting her with whatever was in his hand.

There were no windows and no other way out.

There was nothing nearby for her to throw at him, and if they had hand-to-hand combat, there wasn't much chance of Bree winning.

She backed farther into the corner, trying to figure out what she could do, and felt her shoulder get snagged on something.

The fuse box.

It wasn't a great option but it was at least something. No windows meant no power would bring total darkness.

She glanced at the room trying to memorize where everything was. She would have to dive behind the table, crawl and reach for his gun. Of course, he'd probably be doing the same.

Jeter was still talking. The man had always loved the sound of his own voice. "Surely you know we were always meant to be together, Bethany. Tanner said you would run. That you would never come to me, not even to trade yourself for his life. But I knew the truth. You and I, no matter what shape or form these faces end up in, belong together."

Jeter was staring at the syringe, lost in his own words. She knew she wouldn't have a better chance. She snatched open the fuse box, and immediately saw the master fuse. It looked like there was some sort of set of wires hanging off it, but Bree didn't care even if it shocked her.

"No!" Jeter screamed.

Out of the corner of her eye she saw him dive for her. She grabbed the master switch and yanked it over.

Everything went black. She dived for the back of the room like she'd planned.

Then screamed as everything began to explode around her.

Chapter Twenty-Four

Tanner wasn't a particularly claustrophobic person, but trying to keep calm minute after minute inside a casket was difficult even for him.

He wasn't sure why Jeter hadn't used the carbon monoxide like he'd threatened, and at this point Tanner was beginning to think that might be less of a blessing and more of a curse.

Maybe Bree hadn't gotten his message. She had to have been scared out of her mind to interact with Jeter. She wouldn't have known that Tanner knew where he was and that he was trying to signal in some way.

If he was going to die here, he was going to die praying Bree had done the smart thing and had run in the opposite direction. That she'd made her decisions with that computer brain of hers, and known that there was no way Jeter was ever going to let him go.

A year ago that's what she would've done. Hell, maybe even a few weeks ago. But he knew the truth now. Bree loved him the way he loved her and she would never leave him here to die if there was any possible thing that she could do.

Now he just wished he'd asked her to marry him any of the times he'd had the chance, even if the situation hadn't been perfect.

He began to fade in and out of consciousness. It wasn't so bad. When he was out he could hear Bree's sweet voice talking to him. And sometimes others, like Whitaker and Penelope. Although he'd much rather hear Bree.

"Tanner! Are you here?"

Tanner opened his eyes. Whitaker's voice sounded a lot louder this time.

"Tanner. Call out." Penelope.

"Hey!" Damn it. His voice was too weak. Instead, he brought his elbow as hard as he could against the side of the casket. At least that cheap bastard used wood.

"Everybody shut up. I heard something," Whitaker yelled. "Do it again, Tanner."

Tanner continued to thump. The effort was excruciating. He was definitely running out of oxygen in here.

"I've got him!" Tanner heard something on the top of the casket. "There's a lock. Get something to cut it with."

There was a lot more commotion, and he tried

to focus on that rather than the dwindling air. Finally the casket flew open.

The light was blinding, but the air... Oh, the precious air. Tanner took great gulps of it while Whitaker and Penelope helped get him out of his restraints and sit up.

Somebody pressed a bottle of water into his hands as Tanner took in the scene around him. "You got my message."

"Actually, Bree got your message and then made sure we saw it," Penelope explained. "But we don't know where Bree is. I gave her my car thinking we'd be able to track it, but she changed vehicles for some reason."

Tanner stood all the way up. "Jeter would've thought of that. But he's close by with her. He's set up some sort of headquarters around here."

"If Jeter kidnapped you, then who is the guy in the hospital?" Whitaker asked.

"Somebody willing to lose all his freedom to make sure the real Jeter gets his. It's a plan they've had in place for years. It was always just a matter of time before it was implemented."

"We've got every Dallas PD officer available nearby," Penelope said. "And Jeter is on the top of everybody's most-wanted list, so we can have everyone from the FBI to Homeland Security here within the hour searching for him."

Tanner shook his head. "An hour will be too

late. And Jeter is crazy when it comes to Bree. He told me he set it up so that if he can't have her, nobody will. If we go on a door-to-door hunt, he's going to kill her."

"I can have Jeremy pull up the building plans from around here and send them to us," Penelope said. "There are only so many places where Jeter can keep himself hidden. He's too well-known to be out in the open."

"No." Tanner shook his head. "That's sure to tip Jeter off. He would have some sort of alarm set if someone pulls the building files. That's what Bree would do. And like it or not, Jeter taught Bree a lot when it comes to computers."

"We don't need a computer to tell us what's around here," Whitaker said. "I grew up in this neighborhood. I can provide you with at least a basic layout."

Tanner nodded. A basic layout would get them pretty far. Within five minutes, they'd gotten Whitaker some papers and he'd sketched out a three-block radius of his neighborhood.

"If I was looking to set up shop somewhere I wouldn't be noticed, I'd head to one of these two places." He pointed to two different sections of his crude map. "Either here, which was a pawnshop and shoe repair, but has been deserted for at least half a decade. Or these storage units. A lot of shady stuff happens around there, and no-body's going to study anyone else too carefully."

Either place would probably work for Jeter.

"This is your call," Penelope said. "We can go in stealth, or we can go in guns blazing. If he's in one of those storage units, it could take a little bit of time to find him. He'd have the advantage."

Tanner couldn't disagree with that. "Let's concentrate there. Jeter would definitely want the advantage."

They were out the door and headed toward the storage units along with most of the uniformed officers just a couple minutes later. Tanner was riding with Whitaker when a feeling in his gut stopped him.

"Whit, wait. I don't think this is right. I know the storage units would give Jeter the advantage, but that bastard is so conceited, I don't think he would even consider that he *needed* an advantage."

"You sure?"

"Plus, he's been sitting in a cell for months. I don't think he'd be quick to put himself back in a box with his first taste of freedom."

Whitaker spun the car around right there in the middle of the street. "I'll let Penelope know we're going to check out the pawnshop."

Tanner swallowed a curse. "I could be wrong.

I did spend the last couple hours trapped inside a coffin."

"When it comes to Bree, I'll take your gut feeling no matter how many hours you've been buried."

There was only one car parked in front of the abandoned pawnshop. A white Honda Civic. One of the most popular cars on the road today. And one that would never draw attention. It was the same type Bree drove because it was so nondescript.

"I think she's here. Let's get inside."

Tanner checked the weapon Penelope had given him and the one in his ankle holster. He and Whitaker got out of the car.

"Let me stick my head in," Whitaker said. "If Jeter is in there, he may not recognize me, but he'll definitely recognize you."

Tanner nodded reluctantly and followed Whitaker to the front door. He opened the door without hesitation, keeping his weapon down at his side, looking more like someone interested in the pawnshop that used to be there than a cop.

Tanner waited, letting the door almost close before catching it. If something went wrong in there he wanted to be able to get in quick.

A moment later the door opened again and Whitaker motioned him inside.

It was dark.

"Vacant except for some sort of office in the back corner," Whitaker whispered.

Weapons drawn, they moved quickly toward the office area. The blacked-out windows made it hard to see. But it didn't take them long to hear both a woman and a man's voice.

"That's Bree." Tanner had never been so relieved to hear a voice in his whole life. "I'm going in."

Whitaker grabbed him. "Think. She's still alive, they're still talking. You storm the castle, and things might go to crap quick. Jeter is smart, Tanner. Be smarter."

Tanner nodded. Whitaker was right. They began looking around the outside of the thin walls of the office. Maybe there was a different, better way of getting in than the door.

The entire far side of the wall farthest from the door was lined with wooden boxes. Tanner didn't think anything of them until he remembered what Jeter had said about if he couldn't have Bree, nobody could.

"Whit, shine a light over here for second," Tanner whispered. Whitaker aimed the beam of light at one of the boxes and Tanner pried it open silently. Both of them let out a curse when they saw what was inside.

Explosives.

"Surely, Jeter won't set those off with him still in the building."

"I don't know. He's obsessed with her. He might be willing to die rather than have her live without him."

Whitaker nodded. "Then we go back to plan A. Storm the castle."

Tanner nodded and they moved to the door. "I'll kick it in. You go low, I'll go high."

Whitaker crouched and Tanner was counting down when they heard Jeter yell from the inside.

"No!"

Whitaker's eyes looked up at Tanner in confusion.

Then everything blew to hell.

THE EXPLOSION KNOCKED both Tanner and Whitaker half a dozen feet away from the door. If they'd been over next to the explosives, it would've killed them instantly.

As it was, half the office was gone.

And Bree was still in there.

"Bree!"

It was almost impossible to see any details in the smoke, but the fire was lighting half the space.

Tanner crawled toward the office. To the side he heard Whitaker coughing and moaning like he was in pain, but Tanner couldn't stop—the man was breathing and that was more than Tanner knew for sure about Bree.

He grabbed Whitaker's phone, dialed 9-1-1 and left it on the ground. Hopefully emergency services would send first responders immediately since they'd be able to track the call.

He continued to crawl toward the office, keeping low to attempt to stay out of the smoke.

"Bree!" He made it to the door. "Bree! Talk to me, freckles."

God, please talk to him. Please be alive.

The smoke got even thicker as he moved inside the door. The far half of the office, where all the explosives had been stored was now completely gone. Computer equipment lay in pieces on the ground and burning on a table.

A leg bent at an awkward angle near one of the computers caught Tanner's attention and his heart began to throw itself against his ribs. Was that Bree?

He crawled over, the smell of scorched flesh becoming stronger as he did. He prayed with all his might it wasn't Bree.

It wasn't. As soon as Tanner got to the shoe he realized it was too large to belong to Bree. This was Jeter.

Tanner didn't waste any more time on him. Alive or dead, he'd have to wait.

A bang against a table that had fallen caught his attention. "Bree!"

A cough.

"Bree, I'm coming." He got to his feet, still keeping as low as he could, and ran behind the table.

Bree was there. She was alive. She was moving her hands all over the ground, crying and coughing.

"Bree."

She couldn't hear him between her frantic movements and crying. He touched her ankle and she screamed, kicking at him.

"Freckles, it's me!"

"Tanner?"

"Yeah, baby. Come on. We've got to get out of here."

"Wait, there it is!" The last word turned from a sob to a cough. The smoke was getting thicker.

Tanner crawled closer to her. She was still feeling around for something. Some evidence? Something about Jeter?

She scurried away, fighting him when he tried to pull her back. "Bree. We've got to go. Now!"

He'd never spoken to her in this way, but whatever was going on inside her mind, she needed to let it go. "You're alive. I'm alive. I don't care about anything else. Let's just get out of here."

But she still scrambled forward another foot. "Got it!"

He had no idea what she was talking about, but she was at least ready to go now.

"Stay close to me. We're going to have to keep low."

They rounded the table and Tanner came to an abrupt stop.

Jeter was there—one leg still lying awkwardly to the side—and had his gun trained at both of them.

"Sorry, Tanner. But I did warn you that if she wasn't with me, she wasn't going to be with anyone."

Tanner's weapon wasn't in his hand. He'd dropped it during the explosion. There was no way he'd be able to get to his ankle holster before Jeter shot them.

"Admittedly," Jeter continued. "You did warn me that I'd have to go through you to get to her. Looks like that's true too."

He felt Bree's hand tighten on his side. It seemed so unfair that they would both survive to this point only to die here.

"Michael," Bree said, just loud enough to be heard over the burning.

"Yes, Bethany."

"I'm coming over to you." Bree got unsteadily to her feet. "Don't shoot Tanner. I'm coming to you."

"I have to shoot him. Don't you understand? You'll never be mine as long as he's alive." Jeter pointed the gun right at Tanner's face and Tanner knew with him only ten feet away this time there wouldn't be any cheating death.

Bree took another step closer to Jeter but was still too far away to be able to harm him. "You said I would eventually give this back to you. And you were right. Here it is." She tossed something small in Jeter's direction.

Jeter's attention was splintered as he tried to catch it, forgetting about his injured arm. It gave Tanner the seconds he needed to get his weapon from his ankle holster.

Tanner didn't hesitate. He was firing as he swung the weapon up and in Jeter's direction.

The man died still reaching for whatever Bree had thrown at him. Tanner looked down and saw exactly what it was.

Her engagement ring.

He had no idea how she had gotten it or why throwing it at Jeter had caught him so off guard. And he didn't care. He scrambled forward, grabbed the ring and took Jeter's pulse, just for good measure.

This time the man was definitely dead.

Bree was staring at him like she couldn't quite take it all in. Tanner didn't blame her.

But they were going to have to process later

when the building wasn't burning around them. He grabbed her hand and pulled her toward the front door, now being opened by firefighters. Whitaker was staggering that way too.

They made it outside, squinting against the sunlight so bright after the darkness, sucking in gulps of fresh air. Firefighters led them to the side so they were out of the way.

Tanner and Bree just clung to one another. Too many times today they'd both been sure they'd never see each other again.

"He's really gone?" she finally said against his chest.

"Yes. Forever. You never have to look over your shoulder for him again."

And she would've, Tanner realized. Even if Jeter had gone to prison, she still would've spent the rest of her life always wondering if the shadow behind her was Jeter.

She clutched him tighter. "This is it. Now we're finally able to move forward. No more past to keep us trapped."

Tanner dropped to his knee right there surrounded by firefighters, paramedics and cops. The building was burning, they were both bleeding and smelling like smoke.

He pulled out the ring anyway.

"This should have been on your finger before today, but for whatever happened in there when you threw it at Jeter and he lost all focus, I'm thankful it wasn't."

She looked down at him, her green eyes even more huge in her face smudged by soot.

"I love you, freckles. I know we have things we need to work out, but marry me. We'll figure out the rest as we go."

Her hands stayed clinched at her side. "I know Jeter is gone, but that doesn't change who I am. The things he did to me… The way I had to live to survive… I'm never going to be like normal women with normal expressions of emotions."

"Thank God. You are everything to me, Bree Daniels. Everything I never even knew I wanted. Now say you'll be my wife so poor Whitaker over here can stop pretending like he's not about to cough up a lung."

She cupped his face with her hands. "Are you sure?"

"I've never been more sure of anything in my entire life."

The smile that split her face was breathtaking. "Then yes. I'm yours, forever."

* * * * *

Get 4 FREE REWARDS!

We'll send you 2 FREE Books plus 2 FREE Mystery Gifts.

Harlequin® Romantic Suspense books feature heart-racing sensuality and the promise of a sweeping romance set against the backdrop of suspense.

FREE Value Over $20

Get 4 FREE REWARDS!

We'll send you 2 FREE Books plus 2 FREE Mystery Gifts.

Harlequin Presents® books feature a sensational and sophisticated world of international romance where sinfully tempting heroes ignite passion.

FREE Value Over **$20**

YES! Please send me 2 FREE Harlequin Presents® novels and my 2 FREE gifts (gifts are worth about $10 retail). After receiving them, if I don't wish to receive any more books, I can return the shipping statement marked "cancel." If I don't cancel, I will receive 6 brand-new novels every month and be billed just $4.55 each for the regular-print edition or $5.80 each for the larger-print edition in the U.S., or $5.49 each for the regular-print edition or $5.99 each for the larger-print edition in Canada. That's a savings of at least 11% off the cover price! It's quite a bargain! Shipping and handling is just 50¢ per book in the U.S. and $1.25 per book in Canada.* I understand that accepting the 2 free books and gifts places me under no obligation to buy anything. I can always return a shipment and cancel at any time. The free books and gifts are mine to keep no matter what I decide.

Choose one: ☐ **Harlequin Presents®**
Regular-Print
(106/306 HDN GNWY)

☐ **Harlequin Presents®**
Larger-Print
(176/376 HDN GNWY)

Name (please print)

Address _____ Apt. #

City _____ State/Province _____ Zip/Postal Code

Mail to the **Reader Service:**
IN U.S.A.: P.O. Box 1341, Buffalo, NY 14240-8531
IN CANADA: P.O. Box 603, Fort Erie, Ontario L2A 5X3

Want to try 2 free books from another series? Call 1-800-873-8635 or visit www.ReaderService.com.

HP19R3